Hc

The Walking Kangaroo
Central Island
Ahmed Andridge

Hoppy

The Walking Kangaroo

Central Island

Ahmed Andridge

ISBN: 9781976846519

Table of Contents

Chapter One

The Walk

On an eventful day, Hoppy's heart brimmed with excitement as he readied himself to take a remarkable leap in his young life. Today, he would venture out of his mother's safe pouch for the very first time, and the thrill surged through his tiny kangaroo body like a wild river.

In the cozy kitchen downstairs, the morning sun painted a warm glow through the windows. Hoppy's father sat at the table, engrossed in the morning paper, his reading glasses balanced on the bridge of his nose. The aroma of freshly brewed coffee blended with the scent of breakfast, creating a familiar yet special start to the day.

But today was no ordinary day. His mother understood the significance of this moment, and during breakfast, she proudly addressed his mischievous twin brothers, Troy and Floyd. "Today is a big day for Hoppy," she declared, her voice full of pride.

However, amidst the celebratory atmosphere, Troy couldn't resist injecting a playful tease. "Just don't trip and land on your head, little dork," he quipped with a grin. Floyd joined in, adding, "Yeah, we wouldn't want a less intelligent brother around."

"Mom, they're making fun of me again," Hoppy said, his voice tinged with sadness.

His mother's expression turned serious, and she firmly stated, "I've had enough of this. Stop teasing your younger brother!"

"That's what you said last time, Mom!" Troy interjected.

"This time, I mean it!" his mother affirmed with determination.

"You said that last time too!" Floyd shot back.

"It's time for both of you to get to school," she said, her patience wearing thin.

"But Mom, we're still eating," Troy mumbled with his mouth full.

"I said, NOW!" she raised her voice, making her point clear. Both Troy and Floyd hurriedly finished their meals and rushed to their feet, knowing better than to test their mother's patience further. As they headed towards the front door, their mother reminded them, "Your lunch is by the door."

Troy, trying to play the protective older brother, couldn't resist giving his younger sibling a piece of advice. "Be careful not to fall on your head, little brother!" he playfully warned, holding the door open for them.

"Why? Did that happen to you on your first day?" Hoppy retorted with a hint of frustration. His older brother, Troy, closed the door behind them, leaving Hoppy feeling left out and annoyed. In a moment of childish rebellion, Hoppy stuck his tongue out at them, a playful gesture of defiance.

But his mom was swift to correct him. "Hoppy, put your tongue back in. It's time for you to leave my pouch. Between you and your brothers, I'll need a new back!" she exclaimed, clearly exasperated.

Despite the lighthearted teasing from his brothers, Hoppy's excitement burned brightly within him. With a heart full of anticipation, he readied himself for his very first leap into the world outside his mother's pouch. The challenges that awaited him didn't deter his determination; instead, he embraced them with unwavering enthusiasm.

On the kitchen table, Hoppy's father's newspaper showcased a front-page story about the Earth's momentary axis shift the previous January. He read the article with a furrowed brow, his curiosity piqued. Setting the newspaper aside, he bid his wife farewell and stated, "Off to work."

As the sun ascended, casting a warm, golden hue across the landscape, Hoppy's excitement swelled. The moment he had eagerly awaited was finally at hand. Leaving behind the snug sanctuary of his mother's pouch, he ventured into a day filled with new encounters and endless opportunities.

"Mom, could we please go to the park?" Hoppy asked, his eyes shining with anticipation. "I want my first hop to be there. Can we?"

His mother's expression held a trace of hesitation. "It's quite a distance, and I'm not really up for it," she responded, her voice carrying a hint of weariness.

Unfazed, Hoppy persisted, his tone hopeful. "Please, Mom? You only took me there once." With an attempt to charm her, he offered his most endearing smile, hoping it would sway her.

A pause lingered as his mother contemplated his request. Eventually, she surrendered, a soft grin forming. "Well, your

7

cuteness wins this time," she conceded with a chuckle. "Let's go and seek out some new adventures together."

Overflowing with gratitude, Hoppy exclaimed, "Thank you, Mom! I'm going to make you proud." Inspired by his mother's response, he felt motivated to live up to his words. She retorted, "You better! Your brothers aren't exactly setting the bar high."

The park greeted the early morning with a gentle, golden radiance as the sun painted the surroundings. Dew-kissed grass sparkled like a field of diamonds beneath its tender rays. Trees stood majestically, their branches swaying in the soft breeze that carried the promise of a fresh day. The scene was adorned with a few early risers—dedicated joggers, couples enjoying leisurely walks, and, of course, mothers with their little ones. Among them, Hoppy's mother joined the ranks of caretakers who had brought their young charges out to explore. Each mother wore a story on her face—a blend of weariness, delight, and an unbreakable bond with her offspring. Baby ducks added to the ambiance, their tiny quacks weaving a playful melody into the serene setting. Amid this tranquil backdrop, Hoppy's mother stood, her pouch cradling her precious young kangaroo, ready to introduce him to the wider world.

Assuming responsibility, Hoppy's mother declared, "Alright, Hoppy, time to give me a break. Out you come!"

Overflowing with excitement, Hoppy emerged from his mother's snug pouch. His furry tail twitched with eagerness as he responded, "You don't have to tell me twice! I'm eager to experience freedom too!" His enthusiasm was infectious. With a leap of faith, he embarked on his exploration of the outside world. However, his landing didn't go as smoothly as he'd hoped, and he found himself seated ungracefully on the ground. It was his first experience of solid earth beneath him, and he couldn't resist running his hands over the soft grass blades, a gesture filled with wonder and curiosity.

The sensation of solid ground beneath him brought Hoppy immense joy. He embraced the feeling of independence, ready to discover the marvels that lay ahead.

"I'm finally free!" he exclaimed, his voice brimming with elation.

"Me too! Now, get up from your behind and take your very first hop," his mother encouraged, her words laced with enthusiasm.

"Alright, Mom," Hoppy responded, his resolve unwavering.

With newfound determination, Hoppy rose to his feet and attempted his first hop. To his chagrin, he stumbled.

"Come on, Hoppy, I don't have all day. Start hopping!" his mother urged, a hint of impatience in her voice.

"Mum, I don't think I know how to hop," Hoppy confessed, his tone tinged with uncertainty.

The young kangaroo stood before his mother, eager to showcase his newfound skill. "Don't be absurd, just hop—you're a kangaroo!" she exclaimed. Fueled by his mother's encouragement, Hoppy lifted one foot and took a step, then another, and another. "Look, Mom, I'm walking!" he proudly proclaimed. "I can walk!"

However, Hoppy's elation was short-lived as his mother's tone shifted abruptly. "Hoppy, what are you doing? Stop that at once before someone sees us!" she urgently commanded. A mix of confusion and disappointment washed over Hoppy, prompting him to cease his movements. "I'm sorry, Mom," he murmured. "I'll try again."

In a moment of frustration, his mother exclaimed, "Yes, try again! I don't know what you were doing, but you nearly gave me a heart attack." Driven by the desire to succeed, Hoppy steeled himself and muttered, "Okay, just one more try." With a deep breath, he readied himself for another attempt. As he prepared to leap, his mother's voice cheered him on, "There you go, Hoppy. That's a good start." But instead of hopping, he found himself walking once more.

Amid a blend of determination and disappointment, Hoppy resolved to make another effort. This time, he channeled all his energy into his hind legs, envisioning the quintessential kangaroo hop. With a surge of determination, he propelled himself forward, experiencing the momentary flight that a successful hop provided. "I did it!" Hoppy exclaimed, triumph evident in his voice. "I hopped!" Yet, to his bewilderment, right after he hopped, he transitioned back into walking.

In one swift motion, Hoppy's mother scooped him up, her grip firm on his ears, and returned him to her pouch. Familiar warmth and safety enveloped him, but her words punctured the comfort.

"We must head home immediately! I won't tolerate any embarrassment in public, not today, not ever," she declared sternly.

Confusion clouded Hoppy's mind as he summoned the courage to question his mistake. He found himself seated in the cozy living room of their family abode, surrounded by well-known furniture and the comforting embrace of home. Sunlight streamed through the curtains, casting a gentle radiance on the walls adorned with family portraits and vibrant artwork.

The lingering scent of breakfast in the air served as a reminder of the morning's events. "Why is all of this happening?" Hoppy asked, his voice filled with genuine innocence.

His mother let out a sigh of disappointment, sinking into her favorite rocking chair, its soft creaks matching her movements. She gazed out the window, her eyes distant with a mix of concern. "Why am 'I' dealing with such behavior?" she pondered aloud, her tone a blend of frustration and sadness. "Wait until your father hears about this," she continued, a touch of worry tinging her words. Returning her focus to Hoppy, her expression softened as she added, "If your father's colleagues catch wind of this, he'll become the laughingstock. Those game nights with the girls will become impossible if they find out."

The weight of her words hung heavy as they made their way back home, leaving Hoppy to contemplate the consequences of his actions. Deep down, a sense of frustration brewed, stifling his spirit.

As the school day concluded, the twins burst into the house, their energy filling the air with excitement. News of Hoppy's peculiar walking ability was fresh, and their voices buzzed with surprise and curiosity. Amidst this lively scene, Floyd couldn't resist taunting his younger brother. His teasing carried a playful edge, mixing jest with mischief; he even playfully questioned

11

whether they were truly related. With a downcast demeanor, Hoppy settled on the couch, his gaze fixed on the carpet's intricate patterns.

"I always knew we weren't real siblings!" Floyd chimed in, grinning mischievously. Troy joined the chorus, fanning the flames, "Yeah, that's why you're so different, Hoppy!"

Feeling hurt and frustrated, Hoppy turned to his mom for support. "Mom, they're making fun of me again!" he exclaimed, seeking refuge in his mother's reassuring presence.

Yet, as Hoppy stood puzzled, he noticed his mom sitting in her rocking chair with an ice bag on her head. Repeated calls went unanswered. "Mom?" he tried once more, a hint of unease creeping in. The silence hung heavy, casting a sense of unease over him.

Floyd seized the chance to provoke Hoppy. "See?" he taunted, "I told you she's not really your mom!" Although Floyd's words hit hard, Hoppy recognized them as mere provocation, empty of truth.

Just as tensions mounted, the front door swung open, revealing Hoppy's father. After a long day at work, his weary face bore the weight of challenges. His entrance shifted the atmosphere instantly.

"Honey, we're in trouble!" Hoppy's mom exclaimed, rising from her seat to approach her husband.

His gaze darted around anxiously, his voice edged with concern. "Who? What's going on?" His searching eyes shifted, seeking answers.

Her grip on his arms tightened, her despair evident in her tone. "We're cursed. My life is ruined! They'll make fun of me forever."

Confusion clouded his expression as he questioned, "Cursed? What's going on? Who will mock you?"

His mother's voice carried a touch of exasperation as she clarified, "Your own son!"

Curiosity piqued, Hoppy's father pressed for more details, "Which one this time? Which twin?"

Shaking her head, his mother clarified, "Not the twins. It's their younger brother."

With a sinking feeling, Hoppy realized his name was intentionally omitted. Frustration and disappointment mingled as he watched his father peer down at her pouch, asking, "Who? Hoppy? Did he leave your pouch today?"

A wry smile tugged at his mother's lips as she replied, "He certainly left the pouch, but your Hoppy couldn't quite hop. He walked!"

Embarrassment washed over Hoppy like a tidal wave, his attempt to show off his hopping skills had turned into fodder for his family's teasing. The weight of his father's expectations and his brothers' jests pressed down, almost tangible. As tears threatened to blur his vision, he felt the sting behind his eyes, begging for release.

Among the swirling emotions, his mother's hand rose to her forehead, her voice a poignant reflection of defeat. "I'm doomed!" Her words hung heavy with a sense of surrender, as if the situation had spiraled beyond her control.

His father's brow furrowed with a mix of confusion and concern as he sought clarification. "What on earth are you saying? You're leaving me utterly perplexed." He struggled to piece together the puzzle that had unexpectedly taken center stage.

Troy seized the opportunity to clarify, his tone equal parts informative and mischievous. "Mom's saying that Hoppy's got a knack for walking instead of hopping." His words shed light on Hoppy's unique trait, revealing a hidden layer.

Floyd chimed in, a glint of mischief in his eyes. "Yeah, Dad, you might want to uncover his true origin." His cryptic comment hinted at a deeper narrative, inviting curiosity.

His father's gaze shifted to Hoppy, concern etched in his features. "Is this true, Hoppy?" The question hung in the air, a bridge to understanding that awaited a traveler.

A soft sigh escaped Hoppy's lips, a single tear tracing a path down his cheek before settling on his leg. "It's not my fault," he whispered, his voice trembling with vulnerability. As if summoned, more tears followed, punctuating his words with unspoken emotion.

His father's voice filled the room, a storm of disappointment and frustration. "Go to your room immediately! You're grounded until further notice!" The command cut through the air with authority, sealing Hoppy's fate.

Bewilderment crossed Hoppy's face as he spoke a simple truth. "But I don't have a room."

A fleeting softening of his dad's expression signified a recognition of the oversight. "Then go to my office upstairs and stay there," he instructed, a note of sympathy now woven into his words.

14

Climbing the staircase to his refuge, Hoppy was trailed by Floyd's parting jest, a caustic reminder of his predicament. With each step, his heart felt heavier, burdened by Floyd's harshness, yet undeterred in its pursuit of redemption.

But the echoes of his mom's words persisted in his mind like a stubborn echo, casting shadows of doubt. "I am doomed forever," her lamentation hung in the air, a stark contrast to Hoppy's determination to defy such pessimism.

Upon reaching the top, Hoppy entered his sanctuary, shutting the door behind him to find solace in solitude. The door acted as a barrier, shielding him from the world's judgments. Sliding down, he leaned against it, his emotions swirling in a tempest. Tears streamed down his face as the weight of the moment overwhelmed him, the world's heaviness nearly insurmountable. As exhaustion took hold, he surrendered to weariness, descending into an uneasy slumber.

Twelve years had come and gone since the day Hoppy, the unique kangaroo gifted with the ability to walk, became a captive of his own home. The world beyond its walls remained off-limits, leaving him to seek solace and excitement within the pages of thrilling adventure tales. These treasures arrived through a magazine subscription, and Hoppy's heart would flutter with eagerness as he awaited the Mail-Duck, a daily visitor whose appearance illuminated his otherwise confined world. Every afternoon, Hoppy stationed himself by his window, an image of anticipation as he yearned for the sight of the Mail-Duck heralding his much-awaited adventure book.

A sense of joy accompanied this simple yet meaningful interaction that played out through the window. Hoppy's hand would rise in a wave, a gesture conveying his appreciation and excitement through the transparent barrier. The Mail-Duck, a bearer of letters and smiles, would reciprocate the greeting with its own winged wave, wordlessly acknowledging Hoppy's gratitude.

"Your book's here, Hoppy," his mother's voice would echo through the house, shattering the calm. Swiftly, he'd leap out of bed and rush downstairs, the promise of a new literary voyage urging his steps.

"That came quickly!" Hoppy's mom would exclaim in amazement, her eyes curious.

"Thanks, Mom," Hoppy would respond with heartfelt gratitude, his fingers reaching for the fresh adventure waiting for him on the kitchen table.

His mother's nod would convey approval, her hands moving deftly about the kitchen as she continued her chores.

With a heart brimming with anticipation, Hoppy would dart back to his room, the door's closing sealing his excitement. Leaping onto his bed, the bounce of the mattress mirrored his eagerness, and he would dive into the newfound literary world within the pages of the book.

With enthusiasm bordering on fervor, he'd announce the title with exuberance, "The Canoe That Traveled the World." And thus, the tale would unfold, introducing a chipmunk—a creature of small stature yet possessing an unyielding spirit and an insatiable hunger for daring exploits.

From the moment Hoppy's eyes met the captivating narrative, he felt an irresistible pull to dive headfirst into the pages that held the remarkable account of the chipmunk's journey. Enveloped by profound curiosity, he surrendered himself to the tale of a bold chipmunk's quest—a daring odyssey across the vast world in a simple canoe.

Confronted by insurmountable odds, the chipmunk encountered a myriad of challenges. Treacherous rivers, imposing mountains—the obstacles stood as a testament to the chipmunk's resilience and unyielding determination. Yet, undaunted by adversity, the chipmunk pressed forward with unwavering resolve, committed to conquering the world and proving that even the tiniest beings could achieve monumental feats.

As Hoppy navigated the chipmunk's journey, he couldn't help but see reflections of his own life within the pages. Like the courageous chipmunk, he faced obstacles and limitations seeking to confine him. However, he refused to let these challenges dictate his path. Fueled by the chipmunk's indomitable spirit, he felt a renewed sense of purpose—an urgent desire to explore beyond the familiar boundaries that constrained him.

With each turned page, Hoppy's confinement seemed to dissolve. He journeyed alongside the chipmunk, experiencing the thrill of exploration, the triumph over fear, and the resounding victory of resilience through the words of the book.

Amid a lively family dinner, laughter and conversation filled the room. In a fleeting moment of quiet, Hoppy gathered his courage.

His voice tinged with hope, he turned to his father with a birthday wish, "Dad, for my upcoming birthday, could I have a canoe?"

A hushed pause fell over the table, disrupted by a mischievous giggle from the twins. His father pondered, while his mother interjected with a firm yet understanding tone. "Hoppy, remember the rules about leaving the premises. Enjoy dinner and let's not take this further."

Undeterred by his mother's caution, Hoppy persisted, his earnestness overshadowing the warning. But his mother's patience waned, and she raised her voice with authority, "Enough, Hoppy! Go to your room now, and no supper tonight!"

Confusion and hurt swirled within Hoppy as he grappled with the unexpected reaction. "What did I do to deserve this treatment?" he questioned, his voice laden with disappointment. "You never get me anything!" his frustration erupted. Hoppy's father attempted to reason, "You have a world of books in your room, don't you?"

"Books? All I get are books."

Overwhelmed by emotions, his father's patience snapped, "Go to your room!" Overcome, Hoppy's pain-fueled words spilled out, "I wish you weren't my family! It's because I'm a walking kangaroo, isn't it? Just accept it!" Tearfully, he withdrew to his room, the weight of his heart heavy in the air.

In the sanctuary of his room—a space once his father's office—Hoppy embraced his emotions. Tears flowed, sobs echoed, and sleep mercifully enveloped him, offering a brief respite from the ache within.

Morning's tender light kissed Hoppy's face, rousing him from slumber. Blinking away sleep, he couldn't believe his eyes. Just outside his window rested a vibrant, colorful canoe.

Disbelief morphed into elation as Hoppy whispered, "Dad got me a canoe." Overflowing with excitement, an urgent energy coursed through him, pushing him forward. He rushed downstairs, each step resonating with anticipation.

Swinging open the front door, a bittersweet tableau unfolded before him—his twin brothers, Troy and Floyd, standing beside their new, gleaming canoe, expressing gratitude to their dad. "Thanks, Dad!" Troy's gratitude resounded, while Floyd chimed in, "You're the best, Dad!"

A whirlwind of emotions stirred within Hoppy as he observed his brothers' elation. Disappointment tugged at his heart; it was Hoppy who had yearned for the canoe, envisioning his own daring adventures. Yet, the gift had been bestowed upon his older siblings.

Caught in a tempest of thoughts and emotions, Hoppy felt adrift, uncertain of how to navigate the complex currents within him.

Chapter Two

The True Beauty Of Walking

For three consecutive days, Floyd and Troy reveled in recounting their exhilarating escapades with their brand new canoe. Their infectious enthusiasm manifested loudly whenever Hoppy was in earshot. At dinner one evening, Troy's sly remark sliced through the air, "It's a shame you're missing out on all the canoe fun, Hoppy." Startled, Hoppy lowered his fork, locking eyes with Troy, a mix of simmering anger and hurt welling within him. Sensing the tense atmosphere, Floyd added with a smirk, "You should see us when we race against other canoes!"

"You both know I've always wanted a canoe too, but you never paid it any mind until I brought it up to dad," Hoppy retorted, his voice laced with defensiveness.

"That's enough, Hoppy. Finish your meal," his father's firm intervention cut through.

Meeting his father's gaze, Hoppy's frustration boiled over. "What have I done to deserve a family like this?" he questioned, bitterness tinting his tone.

"That's the limit! Go to your room!" his father's patience frayed.

"I was heading there anyway, dad," Hoppy's response carried a trace of resentment. Alone in his room, he reclined on his bed, eyes tracing patterns across the ceiling. A few teardrops escaped, quickly brushed away, his resolve firm not to shed more for his family. Outside his window, the full moon radiated, its glow embracing the world below.

Under night's cover, Hoppy devised a bold plan. He aimed to slip through the window and catch a glimpse of the canoe gliding gracefully on the tranquil river, bathed in the mystical luminescence of the full moon.

Certain he'd go unnoticed, he whispered, "No one will suspect. I'll return before they wake." So, with measured steps, he emerged from his room, becoming one with the night.

On a winding path to the river, his heart raced. Each step brought him closer to the waiting vessel, guided by the moon's silver glow.

Finally, at the water's edge, his gaze locked onto the serene canoe. It felt like it had waited for him, urging him to uncover its secrets. The night was still, leaves rustling and water softly lapping in a soothing symphony.

In this moment's solitude, Hoppy embraced the tranquility and the unbridled freedom around him. The moon's radiant glow painted an irresistibly alluring scene, captivating his senses.

Lost in the breathtaking splendor, he knew this moment would forever stay etched in memory. The canoe's allure and the night's enchantment intertwined, leaving an indelible mark on his youthful spirit.

"Let's head back," he whispered, eyes fixed on the canoe, softly bobbing on water's surface, kissed by the moon's glow. Enchantment woven by the night, he journeyed homeward, a residue of awe dancing within.

Craving solitude, he climbed a tree by his window, but an unexpected misstep disrupted his balance. The resulting turmoil resonated through the night as he tumbled, snapping branches below.

His family poured out, drawn by the ruckus. They found Hoppy amidst the debris, his expression a blend of frustration and dejection. "Oh dear, this isn't good," Hoppy's mother exclaimed, exasperation and concern in her voice. "Do you know how worried you've made us? Inside, now!" She reprimanded, gripping Hoppy's ears firmly.

Indoors, voices filled the room, reproaching Hoppy. "Straight to your room!" their collective admonishment echoed, their frustration evident.

Growing irritated, Hoppy quipped, "If I had a coin for every time I've heard that, I'd be a millionaire!" Annoyed, he retreated, door thudding shut. In his familiar haven, he grabbed paper and began writing:

Dear Mr. Mailman,

I wanted to express my deepest gratitude for the countless moments of joy you've brought into my life with your friendly waves through the window during mail deliveries. You've become more than just a mailman; you're the closest and most cherished friend I've ever had.

Over the years, I've eagerly awaited each package, knowing that within them lie the keys to new worlds and thrilling adventures.

The Adventure books you've faithfully delivered have ignited my imagination and taken me on unimaginable journeys. With every turn of the page, I've traveled alongside brave heroes and heroines, facing challenges and discovering the true meaning of bravery.

Now, inspired by the tales you've brought me, I feel it's time for me to write my own adventure. It's time for me to face the world and embark on my own journey.

With the spirit of adventure and gratitude, I sign this letter sincerely,

Hoppy, "The Walking Kangaroo"

In secrecy, he slipped the letter into an envelope and stealthily put on a crisp shirt and a vest with multiple pockets. Armed with a few essentials, he quietly slipped out of his bedroom window for the second time that night.

Silently, he placed the letter in the mailbox, addressed to the trusty mailman. As the mailbox closed with a gentle click, he couldn't help but mutter words that resonated with freedom and liberation: "The true beauty of walking lies in the ability to escape from this place."

In a moment of disbelief, Hoppy found himself walking away from the dysfunctional family that had caused him so much turmoil. As he made his way to the tranquil river, he couldn't help but reflect on the events that had led him to this point. The night was still and calm, just like the surface of the water that awaited him.

Approaching the canoe, his earlier refuge, he noticed a life jacket within. Safety in mind, he donned it, guarding against uncertain currents. A deep breath, he unfastened the tether, breaking free from his stifling family.

Pushing the canoe from shore, relief washed over him. Troublesome echoes ebbed, replaced by freedom's gust. Long carried burdens lightened, replaced by thrilling liberation coursing through him.

Ahead lay an undefined path, a canvas of promise. Each paddle stroke cleared a trail, leaving behind toxic echoes. The river mirrored his quest, winding like his journey, serene stretches mirroring moments of insight.

Moonlight's dance on water rekindled his connection to the world. Night hummed with opportunity, and he aimed to seize it. Each paddle stroke propelled not just downstream, but through the uncharted journey of his existence. Whispers in the night air held secrets of growth, urging him to welcome forthcoming challenges.

Amid quiet reflection, he murmured, "This is genuine freedom's taste, a night promising a lifetime. I should've broken free sooner." River carried his murmurs, proof of his unburdened spirit leading him.

Time stretched on, hours or fleeting moments. Moonlight dimmed, yielding to advancing somber clouds, veiling the radiant scene with foreboding.

Darkened canopy gathered, his gaze drawn skyward, heart racing. "Rain approaches," he noted, worry underlying his words. Intuition urged action, seeking refuge from the impending tempest.

With determination coursing, he reversed course, guiding his canoe leftward. Eyes scanned the river's edge, seeking sanctuary from the deluge. Each rhythmic paddle brought his haven nearer, water yielding to his resolute effort. His actions echoed his heartbeat, a steadfast rhythm amid the tempest's approach.

Then, heavens parted, rain cascading like liquid arrows. Wind joined the chorus, vying for control. Amid chaos, his determination remained unwavering, a beacon of resolute will.

Rain-drenched and wind-battered, Hoppy clung to his purpose. Solid ground beckoned urgently—escaping the river's grasp before the storm intensified. Elements fought, yet his resolute will blazed, a spark of hope against the tempest's canvas.

Intensity soared, the storm's force shaking his canoe's core. Desperation took hold as he fought to steady it, but nature's grip was unyielding. Toppling, he plunged into churning waters.

Submerged, he battled disorienting currents, lungs craving air. Relief surged; the life jacket aided his ascent. Breaking water's hold, he gasped for air, heart racing with the storm's rhythm.

Against fierce currents, he sought stability, fingers scrabbling for a grip. Grasping rock, he clung tenaciously, defying the river's pull.

Currents raged, a relentless adversary. "Help!" he cried, voice a plea echoing through the night. Each call, a fervent prayer carried by the wind, surpassing the storm's fury.

Perched atop the steadfast rock, a serene frog dozed on a nearby tree branch, oblivious to the unfolding drama below. At the sound of Hoppy's urgent plea, the frog stirred from its slumber, blinking awake and gazing down inquisitively.

"Hold on, what's all the fuss down there?" the frog quipped with an air of nonchalance, its eyes narrowing in intrigue.

Meanwhile, Hoppy grappled fiercely with the river's relentless current. His unyielding determination granted him a firm grasp on the rock's rugged surface, an anchor against the torrent's fury.

"If this turns out to be my first and last adventure, that's just not gonna cut it," he mused aloud, his voice a cocktail of resolve and urgency as he clung desperately to his precarious sanctuary. The storm had abated, yet the threat endured. His anguished plea reverberated through the wilderness once more, "HELP, HELP!"

"HEY!" a sudden interjection pierced the tumult, jolting him from his struggle. Startled, he pivoted toward the unexpected source—a frog, perched on a neighboring stone. "Kangaroo swim time seems a tad unconventional, don't you think?" the frog quipped dryly.

As Hoppy fought against the water's might, his cries for aid rang out in a panicked chorus. The nearby frog, attuned to the gravity of the situation, sensed the need for intervention.

"What a splendid evening," the frog muttered sardonically to itself, dripping with sarcasm. Yet, the urgency propelled it forward. "Listen closely, young one," the frog's tone turned firm. "I'll leap into the river, gather whatever's available, and create a foothold for you. Give yourself a hearty shove once I'm done. But remember, you owe me a favor—one worth my while," the frog's plea was laced with a tinge of desperation.

26

Intrigued and wary, Hoppy considered the offer. "Three favors, and you've got a deal. Just get me out of this mess," he replied cautiously.

With unwavering determination, the frog dived into the river's depths, tirelessly stacking stones beneath Hoppy's feet. The makeshift platform steadied his stance. Drawing on his newfound support, Hoppy propelled himself skyward, emerging atop the rock formation. There, he expelled water from his lungs, the relief palpable as he reacquainted himself with air's embrace.

The frog emerged from the river's flow, hopping over to join Hoppy. Fixing him with an intent gaze, the amphibian's eyes spoke volumes.

As Hoppy wheezed and struggled for breath, he managed a heartfelt "Thank you." Turning toward the frog, still catching his breath, he added with sincerity, "I owe you one."

The frog, quick to correct, quipped, "No, no, my friend, you owe me three. Your own words."

Hoppy nodded, acknowledging the frog's logic. Rising to his feet, water cascading from his form, he affirmed, "You're right. Three it is. So, what can I do for you, Mr. Frog?"

"Greenie," the frog introduced himself with a chirpy croak, the twinkle in his eyes reflecting his cheerful demeanor.

Observing Greenie's brown skin, Hoppy couldn't help but voice his confusion. "But, you're brown," he remarked, puzzled by the apparent incongruity between Greenie's name and his appearance.

Greenie chuckled softly, his response tinged with amusement. "My dad had a knack for irony, I guess. Sometimes, things aren't quite what they seem."

As their conversation continued, Hoppy's intrigue deepened. "So, what's your first favor, Greenie?" he inquired, eager to delve into his companion's requests.

Greenie's eyes glinted with mischief as he responded, "First, kangaroos are famed for their swift hops. To reach my destinations in a jiffy, I need your legs to do the job." A flutter of his tiny webbed feet conveyed his eagerness.

However, Hoppy found himself in an unusual predicament. "Sure thing, Greenie, but here's the catch," he admitted. "I can't hop."

Greenie, taken aback by this revelation, responded with an incredulous quirk of his brow. "Hold on a minute. You're a kangaroo! It's, like, your thing. No escaping this one."

Feeling compelled to set the record straight, Hoppy defended himself, clarifying, "I'm not trying to shirk my duties or anything."

Perplexed, Greenie prodded for more information. "But if you can't hop or swim, how on earth do you get around?"

Hoppy's confession lingered in the air, leaving Greenie in disbelief. "This one's a doozy," Hoppy declared with a mix of amazement and resignation. "I'm a walking kangaroo." Each graceful step he took demonstrated his distinctive mode of movement, captivating Greenie's attention. The look of astonishment on Greenie's face was unmissable; his eyes widened as he struggled to process what he was witnessing. "Well, color me surprised," Greenie muttered, clearly taken aback.

Apologizing for the unexpected revelation, Hoppy reassured his newfound friend, "I'm sorry, Greenie. But even though I can't hop, I can still lead the way on foot."

Greenie's response brimmed with good-natured humor. "I suppose I don't have much choice, do I? It's not every day I come across a kangaroo with a three-favor debt to repay."

Curious about the journey ahead, Hoppy inquired, "When do we set off?"

"It's getting late now, so let's take a breather tonight and start fresh at sunrise. By the way, what's your name?" Greenie quizzed, eager to learn more about his unique companion.

"My name is Hoppy," he exclaimed with an undercurrent of excitement.

"I'm not even going to bother asking," Greenie retorted, a playful glint in his eyes.

Curiosity ignited within Hoppy, prompting him to probe further. "Where's your home, Greenie?"

A wistful note crept into Greenie's reply. "My home has been stripped away."

Empathizing, Hoppy offered his condolences. "I'm truly sorry to hear that. And where do we bed down for the night?"

Greenie's response carried an enigmatic air. "Look around you, find a spot. That's your sleep chamber tonight."

Taking in his surroundings, Hoppy's eyes widened. "Oh my, this is quite the vast bedroom!"

"Rest easy, you quirky kangaroo. I'll rouse you with the dawn," Greenie declared, ascending a nearby tree.

Beneath the tree's welcoming shade, Hoppy slipped into peaceful slumber. A gentle tap on his forehead brought him back to the waking world. It was Greenie, brimming with energy and ready for the new day.

"Rise and shine, anyone home?" Greenie's voice playfully echoed, accompanied by a knock on Hoppy's noggin. Blinking his eyes open, Hoppy found himself face to face with his newfound companion.

"Good morning," Hoppy mumbled, still transitioning from the realm of dreams. "What culinary delights await us for breakfast?"

"Morning munchies? Let me grab the options," Greenie responded with a hint of sarcasm.

"Are you seriously suggesting we have a menu?"

"Of course, we do!" Greenie quipped, his eyes sparkling mischievously. "I've got quite the selection for you today. We've got some freshly picked riverbank weeds, a medley of dew-kissed leaves, and, if you're feeling really adventurous, a handful of juicy insects."

Greenie's laughter echoed through the air, a melody of mischief. "Nah, just messing with you. We'll chow down on whatever grabs our attention along the journey. Now, spill the beans. You ain't exactly a local, huh?"

"You've got it right," Hoppy replied, a touch of sadness tugging at his words. "I come from Darkston, on the other side of the river."

Recognition flickered in Greenie's eyes. "Darkston? Been through there once. But what's the story for you ending up in this neck of the woods?"

With a sigh, Hoppy let his words flow. "I decided to ditch my old life and set off on my own adventure. My family? Well, they're not exactly my fan club. They've got a real issue with me walking – or rather, not hopping. I'm an embarrassment to them."

Sharing his recent struggles, Hoppy continued, "I thought I'd try canoeing, you know, something daring. But then this wild storm blindsided me, flipped the whole canoe. I was scared out of my wits." Gratitude gleamed in Hoppy's eyes as he looked at Greenie. "And then you swooped in, saved my life."

Understanding dawned on Greenie's face. "I feel you." After a quiet moment, he added, "Friends, you choose. Family? Luck of the draw."

With Greenie nestled cozily on Hoppy's shoulder, the two friends hatched a plan. Greenie spoke up. "Let's head west. Yeah, a walking kangaroo might turn some heads at first, but trust me, it's the ultimate cool move."

Hoppy's face brightened. "Man, that's probably the most uplifting thing someone's said about my walking. Thanks! So, where exactly are we headed?"

"I've got to make it to an island – used to be my home. There are some friends there, and it's urgent that I see them."

"Why are you so far from home?" Hoppy's curiosity was ignited like a blazing fire.

Greenie's voice held a resolute tone. "I was on the trail of a witch, seeking her help. But fate had other plans – she got snatched by pirates."

Hoppy's disbelief was painted all over his face. "Wait a sec! Witches are for real?"

"As real as you and me," Greenie affirmed, a playful glint in his eye.

"Are they all wicked?"

Greenie chuckled. "Nah, they're a mixed bunch, like any crowd. Not every witch goes around casting evil spells."

They trudged forward, hunger gnawing at their insides. The air filled with an enchanting melody, a captivating tune that momentarily swept Hoppy and Greenie into a different realm. But the music couldn't appease their growing hunger, for there was little to munch on in their surroundings.

Hoppy's eyes lit up with wonder as he couldn't contain his admiration. "That song is something else!" Greenie nodded in agreement, adding, "That bird's got a serious talent."

Almost as if summoned by their thoughts, a striking canary with brilliant yellow feathers descended gracefully before them, exuding an otherworldly aura. With a hint of playfulness, the canary broke the silence, asking, "Enjoying my tunes, I see?" Taken aback, Hoppy couldn't help but ask, "So, it was you?"

The canary flaunted his impressive vocal range, leaving no doubt about his identity. "Your praise is much appreciated," Greenie said. "Some say I'm one of a kind," boasted the canary, his pride showing. "I've even graced the illustrious stage of La Scala, you know." He leaned in eagerly, "Want a taste of more?"

"We're all ears," Hoppy eagerly responded. With a graceful wing gesture, the canary declared, "But a melody like mine comes with a price, you know."

"Seriously? Get lost," Greenie's irritation was palpable.

Still wing extended, the canary persisted, "Last chance, folks!"

Greenie rolled his eyes and muttered, "Unbelievable! Come on, Hoppy, let's move on."

Undeterred by the bird's antics, Hoppy pushed forward and shot back, "Move aside, feathered troublemaker."

Clearly amused, the canary chirped, "A walking kangaroo? Now that's a sight! Suit yourselves then." And with that, he soared into the sky, leaving them behind.

"What a sly trickster!" Greenie exclaimed, a mix of wonder and annoyance in his voice. As if in response, eerie sounds echoed from the towering trees above, growing more unsettling by the moment. Trying to keep their composure, they brushed off the discordant notes. But Greenie's patience wore thin, and he bellowed, "Enough! Silence!"

Out of nowhere, as if summoned by their desire, the brilliant canary gracefully descended and settled before them once more.

"Did you just command silence?" the canary chirped.

"YES!" they both exclaimed in unison, a surge of relief coursing through them.

"Well then, you better make it worth my time!" the canary replied, extending its wing with a sense of anticipation.

33

"You won't get a single thing from us!" they both retorted in unison again, determination in their voices.

"Fine," the canary relented, its beak opening to emit those jarring, cacophonous noises once more. High above, a magnificent eagle soared elegantly, its sharp eyes scanning the surroundings. Suddenly, its attention was captured by the melodious canary, pouring its heart into song. Swift as lightning, the eagle descended with precision, snatching the canary from the air and gripping its delicate form in its powerful beak. With a burst of power, the eagle ascended skyward, carrying its prize away.

Caught off guard, the canary let out a muffled cry, "Help, help!"

Without a moment's hesitation, Hoppy sprang into action, charging forward in the very path the eagle took. Each bound quickened his pace, the rush of air against his fur a testament to his determination. Greenie held tight to Hoppy's shoulder, bracing for the chase ahead.

"I've got visual on them!" Hoppy's voice echoed with unwavering resolve.

"All I see are obstacles!" Greenie's view was obscured as they raced forward.

Hoppy surged forward with astonishing speed, his kangaroo legs propelling him like a whirlwind. Greenie looked upward, their pace matching and then surpassing the soaring eagle's. But sudden danger emerged. Greenie's voice rang out in alarm, "Hoppy, look out! A tree dead ahead!"

In a split second, Hoppy scaled the tree, its branches bending like blades of grass under his swift assault. The limbs cracked and snapped beneath his kinetic force, splintering as he ascended. "Easy there! I'm not ready to become bird food!" Greenie's grip tightened, holding on amidst the rapid ascent.

Unperturbed, Hoppy reached the tree's zenith. "I might meet my maker today!" Greenie's words trembled with anxiety, unheard in the rush of the moment. Then, in a fluid motion, Hoppy launched himself from the tree's peak, propelled by sheer determination.

With Greenie firmly on Hoppy's shoulder, they glided alongside the majestic eagle, their quarry now ensnared by its talons instead of its beak. "What the...?" The eagle's astonishment was evident as it caught sight of a kangaroo soaring beside it.

"Hey, frog! How about a quick blink?" the cheeky canary piped up.

Greenie's understood and his tongue shot out at impressive speed, aimed for the eagle's keen eye. The impact reverberated through the eagle, a cry of pain escaping its beak as it involuntarily released the canary from its grasp.

Triumphantly, the canary exulted, "I'm free at last!"

Amid the joy, Greenie's voice rang out urgently, "But how do we land?" The weight of their situation was palpable in his tone. Hoppy responded, "Haven't quite worked that part out yet." As gravity tugged at them, they knew they needed a solution – and quickly.

Greenie's words carried a chilling note, "My destiny's getting awfully close." The eternal optimist, Hoppy countered, "Stay positive, my buddy!" Just as a graceful landing seemed imminent, fate played its hand. Hoppy somersaulted in midair, landing with

35

an inelegant thud amidst a tangle of branches. Though cushioned, the landing still brought its fair share of discomfort.

"Ouch, ouch!" Hoppy's cry echoed as they descended, gradually fading as they finally reached solid ground. The impact left him breathless, struggling for air as he lay there. "You okay, Hoppy?" Greenie settled on Hoppy's chest, worry etched across his features.

"Barely... can't catch my breath," Hoppy wheezed. Greenie hopped off, allowing Hoppy to sit up. "Take slow breaths," Greenie advised, and Hoppy followed suit, gradually regaining his rhythm.

Hoppy winced, his body a canvas of aches. Greenie's concern was evident as he took in Hoppy's condition. As they started to recover, the canary swooped down before them once more. "You sure sprinted like a whirlwind. Name's Rocco," the canary introduced himself.

Greenie, irritation clear in his voice, retorted, "Well, Rocco, how about repaying the favor for saving your feathers?" Rocco's response came with a sly grin, "You might've wanted to ask before swooping in to rescue me."

Chapter Three

Gold

"Hey, can I join you guys?" Rocco chimed in, radiating enthusiasm.

"Save your breath and buzz off," Greenie dismissed him with a nonchalant wave of his tiny webbed hand.

"Hold up a sec," Hoppy interjected, his stomach roaring like a ravenous beast. "I'm famished after all that dashing around."

Greenie grumbled in agreement, "Yeah, I could go for a hearty meal myself."

"I've got just the solution. Let me tag along, and I'll lead you to a fantastic feeding spot," Rocco offered earnestly.

"Bocco, right?" Greenie teased, a mischievous glint in his eye.

"It's Rocco," the canary corrected, a hint of irritation creeping into his voice.

"I couldn't care less about your name. We should've left you to the eagle's appetite. Now take off," Greenie retorted sharply.

"You both seem like you could use a snack," Rocco observed, his keen eyes on them.

"My stomach seconds that notion," Hoppy admitted, patting his belly with a wry smile.

After a begrudging debate, Greenie reluctantly yielded to Hoppy's persuasive appeal. The allure of sustenance proved hard to resist, though he emphasized that their main goal was food.

Following Rocco's lead, they embarked on their shared adventure, Greenie seizing the chance to address Hoppy's newfound burst of speed.

"Seriously, Hoppy, that sprint blew my mind. Who knew you had that kind of velocity?" Greenie's admiration rang clear in his voice.

"Believe me, I was just as shocked as you are," Hoppy confessed, a touch of pride coloring his words.

"At least now we can make our way quicker than a lightning bolt," Greenie noted, a renewed urgency in his tone.

"Truth be told, all that dashing turned me into an insatiable muncher," Hoppy admitted with a chuckle.

"You burned off a ton of energy with that dash. No wonder your stomach's sending out distress signals," Greenie quipped, his froggy wisdom on display.

"Hey, you two, whispering back there? No secret mockery of my style, okay?" Rocco interjected, his tone a mix of curiosity and defensiveness.

"No worries, Rocco. We've got bigger fish to fry," Hoppy assured him, dismissing any concerns about jests.

Greenie couldn't resist a playful jab, his voice laced with amusement. "But, Rocco, your walk could give any supermodel a run for their money." Laughter floated in the air, a soothing harmony that seemed to melt away any tension.

Rocco's comeback was swift, his words carrying across the space with a blend of mock offense and genuine annoyance. "Hey, you two, just so you know, I've got ears!"

Trying to lighten the mood, Hoppy chimed in, "Hey Rocco, if your walk is a concern, why not give those wings a workout and take to the skies?"

Rocco's reply held a hint of regret, "I'd love to, but my wing got a little roughed up in that eagle showdown. Got a parting gift from him before he let me go."

Amid the chuckles, Greenie painted a vivid mental picture for Hoppy. "Just picture that tiny canary throwing punches at a massive eagle! Who would've thought?"

The absurdity of the image triggered another round of laughter from both Greenie and Hoppy. Rocco, never one to back down, chimed in defensively, "You know, if you hadn't jumped in, I had that eagle in the bag!"

Quick-witted as always, Greenie countered, "Yeah, maybe as a snack. That eagle could've had you as a light appetizer."

Unfazed, Rocco puffed out his chest and proclaimed with unwavering confidence, "You guys haven't seen the half of it. I'm a karate champ, I'll have you know."

Amusement danced in Greenie's eyes as he responded, "You're definitely one of a kind, Rocco. But let's stay focused. Where's this feast you've been raving about? We've been walking forever."

Rocco's certainty wavered slightly as he replied, "We're getting close, I promise. The grub should be around the corner."

With a puzzled expression, Hoppy glanced at Rocco. "Do you actually know where we're headed, or are we wandering blindly?"

A mischievous grin tugged at Rocco's beak as he answered, "I know exactly where the food is. Just didn't mention how long it would take to get there."

Greenie's disappointment was palpable as he shook his head. "We should've known better than to trust you."

A weary sigh escaped Hoppy's lips as he groaned, "I'm so tired of walking. My legs are about to stage a rebellion."

Rocco nodded empathetically. "Believe me, I'm right there with you."

Their shared frustration resonated, and both Greenie and Hoppy shot Rocco a glare that conveyed their annoyance loud and clear.

Rocco's voice cut through the tension, tinged with concern as he observed their weariness. "You guys are feeling it, no doubt. Your expressions say it all. Take a break, chill out," he suggested, a rare hint of compassion in his tone.

Feeling the tug of hunger and the weight of exhaustion, Hoppy made the decision to take a short break. "You're right, Rocco. Greenie, I'm going to rest for a bit. I'm not banking on Rocco's sense of direction to find food, so I'll just relax here," Hoppy declared, finding a cozy spot to settle down.

Recognizing the wisdom in allowing Hoppy some rest, Greenie nodded in agreement. However, as Hoppy settled down, a spark of excitement lit up Greenie's eyes. "Hang on a second," he burst out, his voice brimming with enthusiasm. "I think I just spotted an apple tree over there," he announced, pointing towards a distant cluster of trees.

Rocco, never one to miss a chance, let his competitive nature take the lead. "I saw it first! Where is it?" he exclaimed, his eyes darting around as he scoured the surroundings for the elusive apple tree. "You can't make this stuff up," Greenie remarked with an amused shake of his head.

Once they reached the apple tree and gathered a few ripe fruits, Hoppy wasted no time sinking his teeth into a crimson apple, his eyes lighting up with delight. "These apples are pure heaven!" he proclaimed between mouthfuls.

Greenie, savoring the flavors as well, nodded in hearty agreement. "You're not kidding."

Rocco couldn't resist seizing the chance to gloat. "Told you I had the inside scoop on some grub."

Mid-bite, Hoppy couldn't help but praise Rocco's knack for finding food. "You're quite the character, Rocco. Unpredictable, but entertaining."

Rocco, as quick with his words as ever, shot back with a grin, "And you, my kangaroo friend, are quite the spectacle."

Laughter bubbled up from Hoppy and Greenie, their camaraderie shining through in their shared amusement. "We're just here to spread the joy, Rocco," Hoppy managed to say, even though his mouth was still half full.

Sated and in better spirits, the trio decided it was time to wrap up the day's events. As the sun dipped below the horizon, stretching their shadows long, they made preparations to light a fire before the encroaching darkness swallowed them whole. "Hoppy, gather some firewood. Rocco, find some dry moss; it's great for tinder," Greenie instructed.

Rocco, always eager to flaunt his abilities, responded with a dash of self-importance. "Watch and learn, I'll be back in a flash. They don't call me the speedster of both east and west for nothing!" With those words, he darted off to collect the tinder, the twilight landscape his playground.

"In all my years observing various creatures, that bird stands out as quite the intriguing character," Greenie mused, his gaze following the fading light on the horizon.

"I'll trust your judgment. I haven't had many chances to interact with animals. Honestly, you're the first real friend I've ever had," Hoppy admitted, a hint of vulnerability in his words.

"I'm honored to be your friend, Hoppy. But before night takes over, could you gather some firewood?" Greenie redirected their focus to the task at hand.

In no time, they gathered the necessary materials for a fire. Guided by Greenie's know-how, Hoppy neatly arranged the wood. Meanwhile, Rocco returned with dry moss, receiving his next job from Greenie. "Hoppy, rub these two pieces together. Rocco, use your wings to coax a breeze and direct it at the moss."

With Hoppy diligently rubbing the stick against the moss and Rocco skillfully using his wings to guide the airflow, a faint wisp of smoke began to rise. Gradually, the smoke thickened, until, like a promise fulfilled, a small flame ignited. Each passing moment fed its growth until the blaze danced and flickered, casting a warm, golden glow.

"That's incredible! Teamwork really paid off," Hoppy marveled, his eyes locked on the entrancing dance of flames.

"We're like the three Musketeers," Rocco cheered, his voice vibrant in the fire's glow.

Greenie, grounded in realism, interjected, "Let's not get carried away, Rocco."

The determined bird defended his role, his pride shining through. "Say what you want, but without me, you'd be hungry and cold. I played a vital part in getting us food and starting this fire."

Their laughter, pure and unrestrained, filled the clearing as Hoppy and Greenie shared another light moment at Rocco's expense.

"Once again, you guys are teasing me! If you're ever hungry again, I suggest you figure it out yourselves," Rocco retorted.

Laughter erupted, the camp echoing with their amusement as Rocco became the target of their jests. "You're all merciless!" Rocco declared, his mock indignation contrasting with the playful smile on his beak. Swiftly, he carved a slice of apple, skewered it on a stick, and held it over the crackling flames. His small act of culinary creativity stood as his defiant response.

"We're sorry, Rocco. It's not our fault your sense of humor is infectious. But what's cooking over there?" Hoppy asked, traces of laughter lingering in his voice.

Rocco's eyes twinkled with mischief as he shared a memory, "When my siblings and I were fledglings, our mother would give each of us a stick with an apple slice. We'd hold it over the fire for a bit, and like magic, it would turn into a delicious treat that tasted like applesauce. So, feel free to laugh all you want."

In those words, Hoppy found a deep connection. He remembered the days of his youth, when his brothers' taunts had stung, each word a blow to his pride. Yet, in Rocco's playful actions, he found a comforting friendship, something he had long yearned for. These thoughts flooded his mind, helping him truly appreciate Rocco's choice to stand by him.

"No, Rocco, we're not making fun of you; we're cherishing every moment with you. Your mom's trick is pretty neat. Can you teach us?" Hoppy's curiosity was genuine.

Eager for new experiences, Greenie joined in, "Yeah, that looks tasty. Can you show me too, Rocco?"

Rocco, adopting an exaggerated air, replied, "If you two dare to venture into the realm of this culinary art, be prepared for a challenge unlike any other. Crafting apple sauce on a stick demands unwavering focus, impeccable timing, and a hint of magic."

Excitement radiated from Hoppy as he reassured Rocco, "Every word has our attention, Rocco. We're up for this culinary journey."

Fully invested, they embraced Rocco's guidance, immersing themselves in the world of apple sauce on a stick with unwavering determination. In the midst of shared camaraderie and a joint effort, their connection deepened. Laughter harmonized as they savored their creation, the apple sauce on a stick becoming a symbol of their newfound unity. Under the starlit sky, their bond flourished in the warmth of the fire and the sweetness of their shared achievement.

As the night deepened, Greenie's seasoned instincts nudged them to consider the hour. "For an old frog like me, it's getting quite late," he suggested, hinting that their fun might need to wind down.

Feeling the weight of the day, Hoppy agreed, "I'm pretty drained after all that's happened. I think it's time to call it a night."

Rocco, recognizing his own exhaustion, chimed in, "I can't stay up much longer either. Today was a whirlwind."

With a last look at the fading embers, the trio settled into their chosen spots, each surrendering to slumber. The campfire's glow dimmed, night spread across the sky, and Rocco's soft snores created a comforting lullaby, soothing them into rest.

Under the starlit canopy, the night enveloped them in serene sleep. But the tranquility was broken by a stirring—a gentle disturbance that awakened Rocco from his dreams. His eyes blinked open, alert to the night's subtleties. Whispers danced through the swaying grass, and rustling sounds composed a mysterious symphony.

"I heard something," Rocco mumbled, his voice barely audible. Alert and curious, he stood up, cautiously advancing into the darkness. Every step was deliberate, a calculated movement filled with anticipation. Guided by faint echoes, he drew nearer, captivated by the enigmatic voices that lingered in the air.

From his concealed vantage point, Rocco witnessed a scene unfolding before him. Two figures engaged in conversation, their words punctuating the silence. The breeze carried their words to Rocco's ears as he listened intently, an unseen observer.

"Did you hear that, Looney?" one voice asked, tinged with unease.

A second voice, assured yet slightly exasperated, replied, "Calm down, Moroony. It's probably just the night playing tricks on your nerves. We're safe here, and sounds are normal."

Moroony's voice, anxious still, persisted, "I just hope our boss doesn't find out a bag is missing."

Looney's tone was dismissive yet steady, "He won't. Let's focus on what we're doing. Help me dig. This spot seems right for our return."

In the shroud of night, Rocco observed their actions. With determination, the raccoons dug, their paws striking the earth with purpose. Secrets hid in the night, and Rocco watched the scene unfold.

"I think this should do, Moroony. Now, where's the gold?" Looney's voice broke the stillness.

A surge of excitement coursed through Rocco at the mention of gold. "Gold?" he whispered to himself, captivated by the revelation.

Startled, Looney turned his head, scanning the night. "Did you hear something, Moroony?" he questioned, doubt in his voice.

Then, a sharp cry echoed through the air, the sound stretching across the sky. Moroony's voice turned urgent, "Let's go, Looney! Quick, stash the bag in the hole."

In a flurry, the raccoons hurriedly buried their secret before fading into the night. But Rocco had different plans. With a swift leap, he emerged from hiding, landing gracefully by the concealed pit. His eyes gleamed with determination, capturing the spark of hidden treasure.

"Gold," he declared, his voice filled with triumph beneath the shimmering stars.

Chapter Four

I'll Share It Anyway

Rocco hovered above the hidden pit, his wings twitching with anticipation. He cleared the thin layer of dirt covering the hole, struggling to lift the bag from its underground sanctuary. Despite its size, the bag proved strangely heavy, defying the laws of physics. "Deceptive little thing," he thought, "it's like lifting a mountain!"

With caution, he unzipped the bag's opening, a gasp of awe escaping him as he glimpsed the concealed treasure. A cascade of golden coins spilled out, glinting in the moonlight. His eyes widened, heart racing with exhilaration. "I'm rich!" he declared, euphoria surging through his veins, as if the stars were applauding his newfound wealth.

Taking a deep breath, Rocco selected a handful of coins, securing them beneath his wing. The weight of the coins against his feathers was a tangible reminder of the life-changing moment he had stumbled upon. Fueled by this newfound fortune, he summoned his determination, lifting the bag from its earthen hiding place. Every step was a struggle, but he refused to yield, carrying his precious cargo back to camp.

Meanwhile, at the shore, Looney and Moroony hurried, urgency and anxiety spurring them on. Leaving their rowboat on the sand, they dashed toward the shore, fear of discovery pushing them forward.

Moroony voiced his unease, his voice shaky, "What if the boss finds out about the bag, Looney?"

Looney, striving to stay composed, responded firmly, "No more 'what ifs,' Moroony. We need to focus on getting the boat to safety. If we're fast enough, the boss won't even realize we're gone."

Determination etched on their faces, Looney and Moroony pressed on, their footprints vanishing in the sand. Their destination loomed ahead—the rowboat, their ticket away from this daring escapade.

Waves brushed the shore as they approached the rowboat. With a shared leap, they boarded the vessel, oars in hand, ready to row toward a large wooden ship nestled in the moonlit waters.

Moroony's worry resurfaced, his voice laced with apprehension, "But what if he figures it out, Looney?"

Looney's patience wavered, his response tinged with frustration. "Moroony, I've told you already. The boss won't know. Let's just focus on what's in front of us."

"If you say so," Moroony mumbled, uncertainty lingering in the night air.

"Quiet," Looney's voice commanded, a firm yet hushed tone. "Help me secure the boat and get onto the ship. We need to keep a low profile to avoid catching the attention of that crafty crow, Chango."

Their hearts beat in tandem with the rhythm of the waves as Looney and Moroony embarked on their covert journey toward the vessel. Their path was guided by the gentle glow of the moon, casting a pale light on the deck's worn wooden planks.

With cautious steps, the raccoons ascended the thick rope ladder, their paws gripping the coarse fibers as they emerged onto the ship's weathered deck. Moonlight painted an eerie glow, creating stark contrasts amidst the surrounding darkness.

"Do you really believe the boss won't figure out our scheme?" Moroony's voice quivered, their breaths shallow, and hearts racing.

"I'm sure he won't," his brother's voice conveyed confidence yet tinged with uncertainty.

Facing the endless expanse of the ocean, they stationed themselves near the rope ladder, ready to pull it up to prevent any unwelcome intruders. Just as they tightened their grip on the rope, a commanding voice shattered the silence from behind them, "What won't I find out?" The words hung heavily, sending chills down their spines.

Startled, they spun around, eyes widening at the imposing figure approaching. A massive gorilla, its sheer size and strength radiating authority, cast a daunting shadow. Its fur shimmered faintly under the moonlight, adding an air of mystery to its already intimidating presence.

Amid their anxiety, the crow Chango descended, landing on the gorilla's broad shoulder. Its jet-black feathers glistened, and its caw cut through the tension like a sharp blade. "These two little thieves swiped one of your bags, Zunga," Chango's words held a mix of taunting and triumph.

Zunga, the gorilla, acknowledged Chango's revelation with a slow nod, his deep, gravelly voice resonating as he addressed the raccoons. "What are you hiding from me?" His voice carried weight, each word instilling further dread.

As tension escalated, Moroony and Looney stood frozen, their hearts hammering in their chests. The looming figure seemed to grow even larger, his eyes scrutinizing them with an intensity that made their knees weak.

"We apologize, Zunga. We didn't think one bag would make a difference," Looney expressed regret.

"What did you say?" Zunga snapped.

"He means we didn't realize you would notice a single bag missing," Moroony explained.

"Enough! I heard him clearly," Zunga declared.

"We're deeply sorry, boss," Looney trembled as both brothers quivered in fear.

The moon hung low in the sky, its silvery glow casting an otherworldly luminescence upon the ship's deck. Shadows danced and swayed with the vessel's gentle rocking, creating an eerie backdrop to the tense scene. The air was thick with foreboding, as if even the elements held their breath.

A thunderous command erupted from Zunga's massive frame, his voice a tempestuous wave crashing against the night's tranquility. "SILENCE, you imbeciles! What on this planet am I supposed to do with the two of you?" His frustration reverberated through the air, a palpable force that seemed to push against the raccoon brothers.

Chango, perched upon Zunga's shoulder, was quick to fire back, his voice dripping with derision. "Perhaps a quick dip in the sea would clear their muddled minds. Toss them overboard and let the waves teach them a lesson."

Zunga's response was laden with a mix of resignation and weary wisdom. He let out a sigh that carried the weight of countless exasperated moments. His head shook as if to dispel the absurdity of the situation. "Believe me, Chango, I've been tempted to rid myself of these imbeciles long ago. Yet, against all odds, they still manage to fulfill a purpose." His words held a tinge of begrudging acknowledgment for the raccoon brothers.

With a tone that wavered between annoyance and commanding authority, Zunga addressed the trembling duo before him, "Listen up, you two. Despite your imbecilic tendencies, I'll spare you from immediate punishment. But do not mistake this for leniency. You must rectify your grievous mistake. Retrieve what you so foolishly stole from me." His words carried a gravity that seemed to settle upon them like a shroud, emphasizing the direness of their situation.

In the velvety embrace of the night, the campsite lay bathed in the soft glow of a dwindling campfire. Its feeble flames sent playful shadows dancing across the canvas of darkness, painting an ethereal tapestry of light and shade. A gentle breeze rustled the leaves, adding a delicate whisper to the symphony of the night. Above, stars twinkled like celestial diamonds, adorning the night sky with their sparkling brilliance.

Rocco's figure materialized from the obscurity, a shadow weaving through the dimly lit campsite. Struggling with the weight of his clandestine cargo, he exerted every ounce of strength to drag and nudge the stolen bag, each movement accompanied by the clinking of coins tucked beneath his wings.

The metallic melody pierced the stillness, casting an air of intrigue into the quietude.

A short distance away, Greenie lay wrapped in slumber, nestled beside Hoppy. The night seemed to cradle them in its embrace, cocooning them in a blanket of tranquility. Yet, within this hushed serenity, a jarring note emerged—the rhythmic clanging of coins, like a secret melody that defied the night's peace. With one eye partially open, Greenie stirred, his curiosity piqued by the elusive source of the sound.

The nocturnal symphony played on, a fusion of rustling leaves and distant nocturnal creatures, as Greenie's awareness took center stage. Swiftly, he leaned across the gap, his palm finding its target as it connected with Hoppy's cheek in a gentle yet determined slap. Hoppy stirred, his voice tinged with sleep as he mumbled, "Morning already?"

Greenie's words cut through the remnants of sleep's haze, carrying urgency and secrecy, "Hush, and listen. Something's not right with Rocco." Hoppy's senses snapped into focus, the weight of the moment settling upon him as he absorbed the gravity of Greenie's concern. Together, their eyes found Rocco, the enigma at the heart of this midnight drama.

With a grace that befitted his avian form, Greenie rose from his resting place, moving towards Rocco with purpose. The campfire's waning light created a chiaroscuro dance between light and shadow, painting a scene filled with suspense and anticipation.

Greenie's voice cut through the stillness like a knife, breaking the silence with a simple yet compelling "Hey." Rocco, caught off guard by the sudden interruption, emitted a small yelp of surprise. His form materialized from the shadows, his feathers ruffled by both the cool breeze and his startled reaction. "Ah, you scared me," he admitted, a hint of indignation seeping into his tone.

From the cocoon of sleep, Hoppy's voice emerged, inquisitive and drowsy, "What are you doing?" The words hung in the air, laced with curiosity as they sought to uncover the nocturnal activities of their feathered companion.

Rocco's response carried an air of nonchalance, a casual explanation to mask his true intentions, "I couldn't sleep, so I took a walk." His voice held a touch of playfulness, as if daring them to question his motives.

Greenie's eyes narrowed as they shifted towards Rocco's hidden secret. "What's in the bag?" he inquired, his curiosity now firmly piqued. Rocco's attempt at concealment was feeble at best; the bag's presence was betrayed by a slight bulge beneath his slender frame.

A game of cat and mouse ensued as Rocco tried to downplay the situation. "What bag?" he responded innocently, his voice carrying a hint of mischief. Yet, Greenie's observation was sharp, his words leaving no room for pretense, "The bag you're hiding behind you. Don't bother trying to hide it. I can see it."

Rocco's response was laced with a touch of desperation, a feeble attempt to evade the mounting pressure, "Why don't you go back to sleep and pretend you didn't see anything?" His words hung in the night air, a fleeting plea for leniency.

But Greenie stood his ground, his determination unwavering, "Tell me what's in the bag or step aside?" The words were delivered with a firmness that brooked no compromise.

The coins sparkled in the moonlight as they tumbled, a mesmerizing dance of wealth and intrigue. Hoppy's voice held a mixture of curiosity and disbelief, "What's all this?" The question hung in the air, a puzzle that begged to be unraveled.

Unfazed by the spectacle, Hoppy continued his thorough inspection, a final shake of Rocco's form causing the last coin to join its companions. With a deliberate release, Rocco was lowered back to the ground, the truth of his secret now laid bare before his companions.

Rocco's voice broke the tranquility, his words carrying a hint of wonder and possession as he scooped up the glinting coins from the ground, each one a gleaming reflection of the moon's light. "The universe wanted me to have it. It was sent to me," he mused, his tone a mix of conviction and awe.

Hoppy's skepticism cut through Rocco's statement, his voice holding a steely edge as he demanded, "That's nonsense. Now, tell us the truth, Rocco. Where did you get this gold from?" The words were spoken with a determined insistence, a desire to unearth the reality beneath the surface.

With fervor burning in his eyes, Rocco eagerly spilled his tale, his voice a crescendo of excitement, "In a hole, I unearthed a hidden treasure, and I swear to you, it's the absolute truth!" His words painted a picture of adventure and discovery, of secrets buried beneath the earth's embrace.

Greenie's skepticism lingered, an eyebrow arched in doubt as he retorted, "That implies you must have stolen it." His words were a calculated reminder of the implications that Rocco's story carried.

Rocco, however, brushed aside Greenie's doubt with an air of unshakable confidence, "I couldn't care less about your interpretation. The divine powers must have specifically chosen me to discover it, or else they wouldn't have awakened me from my sleep." His voice resonated with certainty, as if he was the chosen recipient of a cosmic gift.

The weight of Hoppy's ultimatum hung heavy in the air, a reminder of the choices that Rocco faced. "If you want to keep hanging with us, then you have to take back the gold you found. You got 'til morning to think it over," Hoppy declared, his voice a mix of firmness and empathy, a testament to the friendship they shared.

Rocco's response was marked by a brooding silence as he gathered the last few coins into his possession. The campsite seemed to settle into a contemplative quiet as Hoppy retreated to his designated spot, ready to surrender to sleep's embrace once more.

Meanwhile, Greenie's thoughts echoed in the night air, his musing a whispered curiosity, "I wonder what he's going to do when he wakes up in the morning."

As the night wore on, Rocco's resolve solidified in the dim glow of the campfire's embers. A stick in hand, he etched a circular boundary on the ground, his movements deliberate and purposeful. Suddenly, a yelp of pain erupted from his beak, followed by a string of "ouches," each one punctuating the air like an exclamation mark.

Intrigued by the commotion, Hoppy and Greenie blinked open their eyes, the source of the disturbance unfolding before them. They watched as Rocco, undeterred by the discomfort, plucked a few of his own feathers and scattered them along the perimeter of the drawn circle. His voice held a solemn declaration, "This will protect me and my precious treasure."

With his ritual complete, Rocco hopped onto the bag, positioning himself as its vigilant guardian. As the night enveloped them, the trio settled into a restless slumber, the crackling campfire and the mysterious bag of coins casting a captivating aura over their campsite.

Elsewhere:

The moon hung high in the sky, casting its silvery glow upon the world below. The night was quiet, save for the soft rustling of leaves and the distant murmur of waves crashing against the shore. The campsite, nestled amidst the lush grass, was illuminated by the dim light of the campfire, its embers flickering like stars on the ground.

Moroony's voice cut through the calm, carrying a mixture of frustration and apprehension, "I knew he would figure it out." His words were punctuated by a heavy sigh, a testament to the inevitability of their predicament.

"Quiet, Moroony! Let's move quickly and grab the gold before Zunga becomes even more furious," Looney urged, his words a hurried plea for action. The urgency was palpable, a reflection of their desperate need to salvage the situation.

They reached the hole with hastened steps, their eyes widening as they found it void of the bag they had concealed. Looney's voice was laced with disbelief as he questioned, "What happened to the bag, Moroony?" His tone was a mix of accusation and frustration, the situation slipping further out of their control.

Moroony's own confusion mirrored in his response, "Why? What happened to the bag?" The words held a tinge of defensiveness, his ignorance transparent in the face of the missing bag.

Looney's patience wore thin as he exclaimed, "Can't you see it's gone? It's not in the hole, you fool." The words were sharp and biting, a manifestation of the stress and anxiety that had gripped them both.

Moroony's retort was equally charged, "Well, where do you think it went, Looney?" His voice wavered with frustration, a mirror of his brother's earlier outburst.

"You're such an idiot. If I knew, I wouldn't have asked you. This is a problem. Zunga is not going to be happy about this," Looney snapped, his tone dripping with exasperation. The weight of their actions and the ensuing consequences bore down on them with a heavy burden.

Returning to Zunga's ship, the raccoons' hearts raced as they stood before the colossal gorilla, their fear mirrored in their expressions. "GONE! WHAT DO YOU MEAN IT'S GONE?" Zunga's roar reverberated in the air, the sound a chilling reminder of his formidable presence.

"We mean the bag containing your gold was not there where we left it. Your bag vanished," Moroony's voice trembled as he explained, a hint of fear permeating his words.

"You two are so worthless. I can't believe I'm wasting my time trying to talk to you two idiots," Zunga's anger was palpable, his frustration a storm that raged around them. His dismissal of their worth was a stark reminder of their insignificance in his eyes.

Chango's swift departure from Zunga's shoulder signaled the beginning of a new twist in the tale. The crow soared towards the beach, his wings slicing through the night air as he circled the area where the hole had been dug. A faint glow caught his keen eyes, the hint of firewood illuminating the darkness.

With a purposeful determination, Chango dived towards the glowing wood, his black feathers contrasting against the faint light. He circled inquisitively, his sharp gaze locked onto the scene that unfolded by the campfire.

Perched on Zunga's massive shoulder, Chango delivered his discovery, "A little yellow canary is sleeping on your gold." His words were punctuated by a mixture of intrigue and surprise, his observation casting a new layer of mystery upon the situation.

Moroony, eager to explain, piped up, "Boss, a canary is a small bird." Rolling his eyes in exasperation, Zunga retorted, "I know what a canary is, you idiot!" His annoyance was palpable, a reflection of his impatience with his companions' lack of wit.

59

Surprised by the revelation of Zunga's knowledge, Moroony stammered, "I didn't know you knew, boss." His words carried a mix of astonishment and caution, as he tread carefully around Zunga's temper.

"Quiet down! Go prepare my boat. Nobody steals from Zunga and gets away with it," Zunga's voice boomed with authority, his declaration echoing over the campsite. His towering figure stood on the deck of the vessel, a symbol of power and intimidation. The raccoons wasted no time, scurrying off to fulfill his command, driven by a blend of fear and urgency.

Zunga, the embodiment of strength and might, took control of his boat with a sense of purpose. His rowing arms propelled the vessel with swift determination, guiding it toward the awaiting shore. His reputation as a force to be reckoned with preceded him, and the urgency to reclaim his stolen treasure fueled his every movement.

Arriving on the shore, Zunga secured his boat with practiced precision. Chango, the cunning crow, guided him with an eerie intuition, leading him to the very location where his stolen gold awaited. The journey to reclaim what was rightfully his had come to fruition.

Zunga pushed aside the undergrowth, revealing his coveted bag of gold, now accompanied by a seemingly oblivious canary. The sight stirred a blend of anger and amusement within him, the dichotomy of emotions playing across his features.

"That's the Kangaroo I mentioned earlier," Chango pointed out, his voice laced with amusement as he relished in the unfolding drama. "I can hear him snoring all the way from here. If he's lucky, he'll keep on snoring. But if he wakes up, he might have to face the consequences," Zunga's warning was laced with a foreboding intensity, a harbinger of what awaited Rocco if he dared to rouse.

With deliberate steps, Zunga approached the slumbering Rocco. His colossal presence cast an imposing shadow, the very embodiment of a predator closing in on its prey. In one swift motion, Zunga seized Rocco and lifted him to eye level, the action startling Rocco from his dreams. Feathers danced in the air, an ethereal spectacle as they took flight from their previously grounded state.

Rocco's gaze met Zunga's, his initial bewilderment quickly replaced by dawning realization. "What the...?" he stammered, his voice a mixture of surprise and confusion as he grappled with the abrupt shift in his circumstances.

"I believe you've taken something that rightfully belongs to me," Zunga's voice rumbled, a low and steady growl that brooked no argument.

Rocco's agile mind worked quickly as he plucked a feather from the air and examined it, a gesture of defiance and contemplation. "All that suffering for nothing?" his voice was laced with a tinge of humor, the absurdity of his predicament evident in his words.

Zunga's grip remained unyielding as he menacingly questioned, "Tell me why I shouldn't break your neck?" His threat hung heavily in the air, a tangible reminder of the imminent danger Rocco faced.

"Release me first, and I will provide you not just one, but two valid reasons why you shouldn't harm me," Rocco's confidence was unwavering, his words carrying an air of assurance as he met Zunga's gaze with unflinching determination.

"Do you think I'm a fool?" Zunga's voice held a mix of skepticism and anger, his suspicions evident in his tone.

"Why would you assume that?" Rocco's counter was delivered with a genuine curiosity, an attempt to navigate the precarious balance between defiance and diplomacy.

Greenie's slumber was abruptly disturbed by the noise of conversation, the realization that something was amiss pulling him from his dreams. Blinking away sleep, he peered through the darkness, his gaze locking onto the unexpected sight unfolding before him. A massive gorilla held Rocco in a tight grasp, the tension between them palpable.

Panic gripped Greenie's heart, and his first instinct was to rouse Hoppy from his slumber. However, the fear of creating a disturbance held him back, and he remained hidden as a silent observer of the scene playing out.

Greenie's eyes widened as he recognized the gorilla's true identity, a spark of recognition igniting in his mind. Memories from the past resurfaced, connecting the dots and painting a clearer picture. Murmuring to himself in a hushed tone, he whispered, "Can it be him?"

Zunga, his curiosity piqued, observed the tiny canary before him, his massive frame casting a looming shadow over Rocco. He couldn't help but wonder just how much harm such a seemingly insignificant creature could cause. As his calculating gaze studied Rocco, an idea took shape in his mind. Could this canary possibly be of any use to him? With a decisive nod, Zunga made his impulsive choice, capturing Rocco in his firm grasp and unceremoniously tossing him into the very bag that held his pilfered treasure. The bag's mouth swallowed Rocco and his precious coins, sealing them in darkness.

Inside the bag, Rocco's voice broke the silence, "Hey, it's dark in here!" His words carried a mixture of astonishment and mild complaint, his natural curiosity undimmed even in this unforeseen predicament. Meanwhile, Zunga's hulking figure began to move, his footsteps guiding him towards the shoreline where his boat awaited.

Once Zunga had faded from view, Greenie's sudden urgency shattered Hoppy's slumber. A couple of well-placed slaps brought Hoppy back to reality, his grogginess lingering. "Hey, is it already morning?" Hoppy's voice held remnants of sleep, his confusion evident as he tried to make sense of the abrupt awakening.

"Nope," came Greenie's succinct response, his tone carrying a note of urgency.

"Why on earth do you keep waking me up before daylight?" Hoppy's annoyance was thinly veiled in his words, a hint of frustration tinging his inquiry.

A torrent of information spilled from Greenie, his words a rush of concern and revelation. "It's that canary again. Zunga, a disgraceful gorilla possesses that gold, discovered the bag with Rocco and imprisoned him inside it," he explained, his words tumbling over each other in his haste to convey the gravity of the situation.

Confusion crossed Hoppy's face as he turned his gaze towards Rocco, still lying beside the bag. "What? We should help him," his urgency was palpable, a genuine concern for their friend overriding any other thought.

Yet Hoppy's plea seemed to fall on deaf ears as Greenie dismissed the idea. "Help him? He got himself into this mess; he can deal with the consequences," Greenie's response was tinged with a hint of callousness, his worry directed elsewhere. "To be honest, he's the least of my worries right now. We have a bigger problem on our hands. Rocco has been kidnapped by a notorious pirate named Zunga, and we're no match for him. If I'm not mistaken, Zunga is headed to the Central Banking Island, where I need to be, but we don't even have a ship to chase after them," his words hung heavily in the air, a stark reminder of their limitations.

Wide-eyed and intrigued, Hoppy looked at Greenie with newfound respect. "How do you know so much?" The curiosity in Hoppy's voice was undeniable, his wonder compelling him to seek answers.

Greenie's smile held a touch of mystery, his eyes twinkling with a mix of knowledge and secrecy. "I just know things," he replied cryptically, leaving Hoppy even more intrigued by the enigmatic crow.

Yet, Hoppy wasn't about to stand idly by while their friend faced peril. A steely determination etched his features as he spoke with unwavering resolve. "I am not going to stand here and do nothing while our friend is in trouble," his voice rang out, brimming with conviction.

A raised eyebrow from Greenie was accompanied by a note of skepticism. "When did he become our friend?" The question hung in the air, an inquiry driven by Greenie's insatiable curiosity.

With heartfelt sincerity, Hoppy provided the answer, evoking memories of camaraderie. "Since we shared our first meal and laughed together," his words carried a touch of nostalgia, a testament to the bond they had formed.

Greenie's expression softened, a flicker of understanding crossing his features. He recognized the truth in Hoppy's words, a shared history that had forged their connection. Yet, his concern remained evident as he voiced a caution. "I'm not going to stop you, but I must warn you that Zunga is one tough gorilla," his words carried an undertone of genuine concern.

A determined smile graced Hoppy's lips as he met Greenie's gaze. "Well, I have my speed. Are you coming?" His question held a challenge, an invitation for Greenie to join him on his daring quest.

Greenie's response was a resolute "I suppose so," as he leaped onto Hoppy's shoulder, clutching on tightly for the upcoming adrenaline-fueled ride. With a burst of energy, Hoppy propelled himself forward, his powerful legs churning the ground beneath him into a blur. The wind howled in their ears as their surroundings became a blur of color. Hoppy's pace rapidly increased until his legs seemed to transform into a pair of propellers, propelling him forward with astonishing velocity. Greenie clung on, his feathers ruffling against the wind, a testament to the exhilarating speed of their journey.

As they neared their destination, Greenie's voice carried a mixture of excitement and urgency, "They couldn't have gotten to their boat yet. With this speed, they should be right… Oh, look! There they are!" His words were accompanied by a nudge to Hoppy's shoulder, directing his attention towards the nearing figure of Zunga, who was closing in on his rowboat. Sensing the imminent threat, Greenie swiftly took refuge by slipping under Hoppy's shirt, seeking cover from their formidable foe.

In a breathtaking display of agility, Hoppy materialized right in front of Zunga with astonishing speed. The sight of the swift kangaroo caught Zunga off guard, his massive form momentarily frozen in surprise. The sheer size discrepancy between the gorilla and the kangaroo was a spectacle in itself, evoking a sense of marvel.

"Hey, how did you manage to get here so fast?" Zunga's deep voice rumbled, a mixture of curiosity and amazement evident as he peered down at the seemingly diminutive kangaroo.

Unaware of Zunga's towering presence, Hoppy replied with unwavering determination, "Let's just say I'm pretty fast. You can keep your bag, but I believe you have my friend. Give him back," his voice was assertive, a reflection of his unwavering resolve.

A sneer curled on Zunga's lips as he retorted, "Do you even know who you're messing with?" His words dripped with arrogance as he launched a swift and powerful punch at Hoppy. But with an uncanny fluidity, Hoppy evaded the blow with an agility that seemed almost otherworldly, his movements mirroring those of a phantom.

Undeterred, Zunga unleashed a barrage of punches, each aimed with precision at Hoppy. Yet, like a nimble dancer, Hoppy danced through the onslaught with grace and swiftness, his body seemingly defying the laws of physics. His movements were a symphony of speed, a mesmerizing display of agility that left Zunga in awe.

"How are you able to move so quickly?" Zunga's question carried genuine intrigue, his surprise genuine as he marveled at Hoppy's extraordinary dexterity.

"Get him, Hoppy! Show him who the boss is!" Rocco's muffled voice echoed from within the confines of the bag, his enthusiasm infectious even in dire circumstances.

"Why don't you release my friend, and we will call it a night?" Hoppy's demand was met with a low growl from Zunga, his patience wearing thin. Rocco's muffled protests only added to the tension, his desperate cries for freedom fueling the mounting conflict.

The atmosphere was charged with anticipation as the confrontation escalated. Zunga's towering figure loomed over Hoppy, his formidable presence an imposing sight. The gorilla's massive fists clenched in frustration, his irritation palpable as he struggled to control the situation.

"You are beginning to get on my nerves," Zunga's grumbled declaration was punctuated by the rumble in his voice, his patience hanging by a thread. Without warning, he unleashed a powerful swing, his massive arm connecting with Hoppy's face in a devastating blow. The impact was jarring, sending shockwaves through Hoppy's body as he was knocked off his feet, his consciousness slipping away.

As Hoppy lay unconscious, Zunga's form darkened the sky above him. With a calculated stride, the gorilla stepped over Hoppy's prone body, his footsteps resounding with a weighty finality as he made his way towards his boat, his bag of stolen treasure now secured in his grasp.

Meanwhile, trapped within the bag, Rocco's voice reverberated with desperation, "Hoppy, you there?"

"Shut up, bird!" Zunga sneered. "Your friend is no longer with us. He went down quick. Hahahaha," his sinister laughter echoed, a chilling reminder of the stakes at play.

Unfazed by Zunga's taunts, Rocco's determination remained unshaken as he sought a way out of his predicament. "I'll make a deal, Mr. Nice Gorilla. If you let me out, I'll share this gold with you," his voice carried a mix of desperation and negotiation.

Zunga scoffed at the suggestion, his arrogance unwavering. "What are you talking about? It's my gold," his words were punctuated by a possessive tone.

But Rocco's resolve was unyielding. "I'll share it anyway," his offer was a last-ditch attempt to gain his captor's favor, a glimmer of hope in the face of dire circumstances.

Chapter Five

The Red Carrack

As the first gentle rays of sunlight began to pierce the horizon, Hoppy's eyelids fluttered open, and he gradually stirred from the depths of unconsciousness. The world around him appeared hazy and disjointed, like pieces of a puzzle waiting to be put together. His head throbbed in response to the blow he had taken from Zunga, leaving him in a state of disoriented confusion. He mumbled softly to himself, his voice a mere whisper carried by the morning breeze, "What happened? Where am I?"

With a slow and deliberate blink, Hoppy's eyes came into focus, fixing on an unexpected and surreal sight. Perched atop his stomach, Greenie maintained an odd yet surprisingly steady posture, his feathers slightly ruffled by the gentle breeze. Holding up two fingers in a gesture both whimsical and oddly practical, Greenie inquired, "How many fingers am I holding up?"

Blinking a few more times to clear his vision, Hoppy responded with a drowsy voice, "Two," his words punctuated by a groggy tone that still clung to the remnants of his dazed state.

The quirky inquiry transitioned seamlessly into a more serious line of questioning as Greenie pressed on, his demeanor both concerned and inquisitive. "Alright, what's your name?"

With each passing second, the fog in Hoppy's mind began to lift, and he answered with growing clarity, "Hoppy," his voice now carrying a newfound strength as he shook off the lingering effects of his ordeal.

Greenie nodded approvingly, his eyes narrowing with focus. "Do you recognize me?"

Hoppy's gaze shifted to meet Greenie's, his response a mix of acknowledgment and weary amusement. "Yeah, you're Greenie. I just got taken out by a huge gorilla who snatched Rocco. I'm okay, no need to ask any more questions."

A sense of understanding passed between them, conveyed in the nod of Greenie's head. "Alright, fair enough. Not everyone bounces back from a punch by Zunga," he acknowledged, a note of respect in his voice. "Many tough pirates have immense respect for his strength and fear him."

Curiosity flickered in Hoppy's eyes, his interest piqued by the mention of Zunga. "How much do you really know about Zunga?"

A knowing smile tugged at the corners of Greenie's beak as he leaned in, his voice lowered as if sharing a secret. "We have a long history together, but that's a tale for another time. Right now, he's headed to the same island we need to be on."

Seeking reassurance, Hoppy voiced his concerns, "What do you think Zunga plans to do with Rocco?"

Greenie's response carried a note of assurance, his words meant to quell Hoppy's anxieties. "If Zunga intended to harm him, he could have easily ended Rocco's life the moment he captured him."

Hoppy's tense shoulders relaxed at the reassurance, and he took in a deep breath. "I reckon the tiny yellow rascal will be alright for the time being."

A determined glint entered Greenie's eyes, his focus unwavering as he outlined their plan. "We gotta make our way to the ship Zunga is on, The Red Carrack."

A flicker of realization crossed Hoppy's face as the name registered. "Red Carrack!?"

A wry grin played at the corners of Greenie's beak, his tone tinged with pride. "I named it The Red Carrack. Apparently, Zunga stole it," he proclaimed, a mix of amusement and audaciousness lacing his words.

The exchange left Hoppy momentarily speechless, his incredulous gaze fixed on Greenie. "What? You gave a ship its name?" he inquired, his curiosity palpable.

A grin played across Greenie's features, his eyes alight with a mixture of pride and playfulness. "Not only that, my friend, but I also designed it!"

Hoppy's eyes widened in astonishment, his mind struggling to process the unexpected revelation. "You designed a ship? Oh, you truly are a mysterious frog! When did this happen?" His eagerness to uncover Greenie's hidden past was undeniable.

The mischievous glint in Greenie's eyes only grew more pronounced as he responded, his tone a perfect blend of secrecy and anticipation. "I'll tell you all about it some other time. But for now, we need to be on it," his voice carrying a resolute determination.

As Hoppy's initial excitement began to meld with a hint of confusion, he pointed out a seemingly insurmountable obstacle.

"But how? We have nothing to sail in, and the ship is long gone by now."

With a reassuring smile, Greenie revealed his clever calculations. "While you were still recovering from the mighty blow of Zunga's Punch, I managed to make some calculations. The vessel has only embarked on a brief journey. They are making their way back to the heart of Central Island. More importantly, the ship is burdened with a substantial cargo of stolen goods, rendering it incapable of achieving its maximum velocity. This ship was built to sail at an average speed of 28 knots, but due to its heavy load, it could only do 15 knots. With your impressive speed, we should be able to reach the vessel in no time. If my calculations are correct, the ship should arrive at the island within a day."

A flicker of uncertainty crossed Hoppy's features, his skepticism evident. "Hey, hold up. How does my speed factor into your plan?"

Greenie's response was both logical and laced with a hint of excitement. "It's actually quite straightforward. Your impressive speed will enable us to run on water. All you need to do is keep those legs moving."

A skeptical furrow formed on Hoppy's forehead. "Do you really think it will work?"

"In theory, it should totally work. But if it doesn't, I can save myself by swimming out of it. However, I'm afraid your life would be at risk because, as we've learned, you can't swim. If you want to back out now, I completely understand. Your life is on the line," Greenie's tone was firm, his eyes locked on Hoppy's, assessing his resolve.

There was no hesitation in Hoppy's response, his determination unwavering. "Not a chance. These past couple of days have been absolutely incredible. You point, and I'll run. But what happens if I start feeling hungry?"

Greenie had anticipated this concern and had a solution ready. "I've already got that covered. We'll bring some apples along with us; you can stash a few in your pockets. Whenever you feel hungry, I'll feed you a couple at a time."

As they gathered the maximum number of apples they could carry, Greenie settled onto Hoppy's shoulder. The moment was charged with an electric sense of anticipation. "Are you prepared, Kid?" Greenie asked, a mixture of seriousness and camaraderie in his tone.

"Absolutely!" Hoppy replied, his voice carrying a newfound determination and excitement.

With a heart pounding with determination, the incredible kangaroo known as Hoppy bounded towards the vast expanse of the ocean. Every powerful stride he took seemed to magnify his speed, turning his legs into a blur of motion. In the blink of an eye, his ordinary limbs transformed into unstoppable whirlwinds, each step carrying him forward with an exhilarating burst of energy.

As the shoreline drew near, Hoppy's focus remained unyielding. With a final, breathtaking leap, he propelled himself into the awaiting waters below. The impact created a mesmerizing spray of droplets that sparkled like diamonds in the early morning sun, casting a veil of magic over his audacious move.

The world seemed to momentarily pause. As if defying the laws of physics, Hoppy's feet touched the surface of the water and, instead of sinking, he kept moving. With each stride, his footfalls sent ripples across the ocean's expanse, creating a mesmerizing rhythm that matched the beat of their racing hearts.

As he gained momentum, Hoppy's velocity reached a level that was almost unfathomable. The water's surface seemed to bow to his presence, bending and curving beneath his weight as he moved forward. And then, in a breathtaking display of agility, he found himself skimming across the surface, defying gravity itself.

The world around him transformed into a watery blur, colors blending and merging in a whirl of motion. Greenie clung tightly to Hoppy's shoulder, his feathers ruffling in the wind as they sliced through the water. The sun's warm embrace and the salty tang of the sea surrounded them, creating an intoxicating sensory symphony that fueled their adrenaline.

Hoppy's heart pounded with exhilaration, the rush of the wind and the rhythmic beat of the waves propelling him forward. The journey ahead was uncertain, the challenges formidable, but in this moment, as he skimmed across the ocean's surface, he felt invincible.

Elsewhere, aboard the grand Red Carrack, the imposing figure of Zunga had confined Rocco within the confines of a small birdcage. Within the opulent private quarters of the ship's captain, a tense atmosphere hung in the air.

With a voice that betrayed his inquisitiveness, Rocco ventured, "Is your name Zunga?"

"Quiet, bird!" Zunga retorted with a sharpness that carried a clear warning in its tone.

Restlessness flickered in Rocco's wings as he nervously asked, "Where are we headed?"

"I am in need of rest. If you dare utter another word, you will face the consequences," Zunga replied with a sternness that left no room for argument as he entered his cabin.

As he surveyed the lavish surroundings of the cabin, Rocco couldn't help but voice his assessment, "This room is so mundane."

Zunga's patience wore thin as he snapped back, "Can't you cease your incessant chatter?"

"This room could use a bit of life, you know. Perhaps some music? Have you got any good tunes?" Rocco suggested, his tone almost playful.

Growing increasingly irritated, Zunga issued a veiled threat, "One more word from you, and I might just offer you as a feast to the sharks."

Rocco, confined within the cage, seemed undeterred by Zunga's menace as he continued his light banter, "Hey, hey, I figured if we're going to be roommates, we might as well get along, don't you think?" In response, Zunga pressed his formidable visage close to the cage, baring his teeth in a display of anger.

Rocco's cool composure remained intact as he casually remarked, "Yikes. When was the last time you took care of those chompers?"

"Silence!" Zunga roared, the intensity of his voice reverberating through the room.

"Alright, alright. I'll keep my beak shut," Rocco replied with an air of nonchalance, though his eyes remained watchful.

As Rocco made himself comfortable on one side of the cage, a leisurely thought crossed his mind, "If it gets a bit chilly in here, how do you adjust the thermostat?"

Amidst his exasperation, Zunga couldn't help but express a mixture of incredulity and frustration, "Remarkable!"

Undeterred by Zunga's reactions, Rocco positioned himself on the opposite side of the cage, getting cozy as he made himself comfortable. With a hint of mischief, he decided to change the atmosphere. Clearing his throat, Rocco began to sing Brahms' Cradle Song, a lullaby with a gentle, soothing melody that floated through the air in stark contrast to the tension that had filled the room.

Zunga lay on his opulent bed, his eyes closed in relaxation, as he allowed Rocco's melodious voice to wash over him. The canary's exquisite song filled the room, carrying a soothing cadence that seemed to lift the weight from his massive shoulders. The gentle notes created an unexpected harmony within his private quarters, a stark contrast to his reputation as a fearsome pirate. However, as the seconds slipped by, Rocco's singing came to an abrupt halt, leaving an echoing silence in its wake.

Zunga's eyes fluttered open in surprise, his imposing form shifting on the bed. "Why did you stop?" he inquired, a touch of curiosity lacing his words.

Perched on his swing within the confines of the cage, Rocco couldn't help but respond with a mischievous twinkle in his eyes, "Oh, so you're quite the fan of my singing, huh?"

A playful grin tugged at Zunga's lips as he nodded eagerly, his tone almost pleading, "Yes, yes, keep singing!"

Rocco's beak curled into an even more mischievous smile as he replied in a teasing tone, "Well, I'm flattered, but I've got to say, my melodious talents come at a price."

Zunga chuckled heartily at the canary's playful demand, appreciating the unexpected exchange. With a hint of theatrical flair, he reached for the ornate drawer beside his grand bed and pulled it open. From within, he retrieved a single gleaming golden coin, its brilliance catching the soft light streaming through the cabin's windows. With a playful flourish, he tossed the coin into the cage, where it landed with a delicate clink against the floor. Rocco's eyes widened in astonishment as he beheld the glistening treasure lying at his feet. In a swift motion, he hopped forward, snatched up the coin, and held it aloft for Zunga to see.

"I've struck gold!" Rocco couldn't help but exclaim to himself, his chest puffing out with a sense of accomplishment. His beak curled into a contented smile as he admired the precious coin.

Without hesitation, Zunga's deep voice rumbled through the room, his enthusiasm clear as he commanded, "Start singing again!"

Rocco wasted no time, his melodious lullaby filling the air once more. The sweet, soothing notes flowed seamlessly from his tiny form, captivating Zunga's attention and gradually lulling him into a tranquil slumber. Soon enough, Zunga's powerful snores became an unexpected part of the room's ambiance, blending harmoniously with Rocco's singing.

As Zunga's snores resonated, Rocco, still singing, cast a watchful eye on the golden coin he held, the intricate patterns etched onto its surface gleaming softly in the light. A daring idea began to form in his clever mind, one that would require stealth and precision. With his heart pounding, Rocco allowed himself to entertain the notion.

Carefully, he halted his singing for a brief moment, his attention shifting to Zunga's slumbering form. Satisfied that the gorilla remained deeply asleep, Rocco resumed his serenade, this time with a calculated purpose. He skillfully used the coin to file away at one of the cage's bars, the gentle scraping noise blending seamlessly with his song.

Rocco's vigilant eyes darted between the progress of his improvised tool and Zunga's sleeping frame, his multitasking skills put to the test. The task was not without its challenges; his delicate wings and small size made the effort taxing, and there were instances when he accidentally halted his singing. Yet, each time his song wavered, the soft rhythm of Zunga's snores acted as a reminder to continue, as if the very sound itself urged him on.

Minutes turned into an eternity as Rocco's determined efforts carved away at the metal bar. A surge of exhilaration coursed through him as he realized that his plan was working. "Just a bit more," he thought to himself, his anticipation heightening with each measured stroke of the coin.

"I can't believe it, I'm actually doing it," Rocco mused silently, his heart pounding with a mix of excitement and trepidation. His passion for singing had temporarily shifted its focus to this daring escape plan, each note now accompanied by the thrill of his imminent freedom.

But suddenly, as if the universe itself conspired to challenge his audacious endeavor, a stern voice shattered the cocoon of concentration that had enveloped Rocco.

"What do you think you're up to?" Zunga's demand rang out, his towering presence casting a formidable shadow within the room.

Rocco couldn't help but feel a pang of annoyance. "Couldn't you have stayed asleep for just one more minute?" he grumbled, frustrated by the unexpected interruption.

Zunga's grip on the cage door was as unyielding as his reputation, and the vast difference in their sizes seemed to emphasize the futility of Rocco's attempt to defend his coin. The gorilla's fingers closed around the gleaming treasure, his determination matched only by Rocco's own resolve. The canary wasn't about to relinquish what he believed he had rightfully earned.

A spark of defiance ignited within Rocco as he clung tenaciously to the coin, his voice ringing out with surprising strength for his diminutive size. "Hey, that's my coin, I worked hard for it!" he declared, his tiny wings flapping with a mixture of frustration and determination. Despite the odds stacked against him, Rocco's spirit burned bright.

Yet, against the sheer might of Zunga, Rocco's efforts seemed almost insignificant. With a fluid motion, Zunga's fingers effortlessly pried the coin from the canary's grasp, asserting his dominance without uttering a single word. The coin glinted in the dim light as it was whisked away, a tangible reminder of the power Zunga held over Rocco's fate.

As if to reinforce his authority, Zunga securely sealed the cage shut, the metallic clank of the door serving as a symbol of Rocco's captivity. The room was once again filled with the quiet ambiance that had been momentarily disrupted by the confrontation.

Rocco's heart sank as he watched Zunga lock the cage, his attempts to regain his precious coin thwarted by the pirate's overpowering strength. The canary's chest heaved with a mixture of frustration and resignation, his tiny form momentarily defeated.

However, Rocco's determination wasn't easily extinguished. With an air of desperation, he implored Zunga, his voice trembling with a mix of emotions, "Buddy, please, just give me back my coin! I promise, I'll stop cutting."

His plea hung in the air, carried by a thread of hope. But Zunga's expression remained unmoved, his attention fixated on something beyond the canary's earnest words. Moments later, the air was punctuated by a familiar call that sent a shiver down Rocco's feathers.

"LOONEY! MOROONY!" Zunga's thunderous bellow reverberated through the ship's corridors, his voice carrying a potent blend of anger and command. In response, the two mischievous raccoons that had accompanied Zunga earlier stealthily appeared at the doorway of the room, their eyes wide with curiosity and a touch of apprehension. The door swung open under their skilled paws, revealing the scene within.

Rocco's heart raced as he glanced at the open door, the raccoons' presence both a potential lifeline and a source of unease. He remained perched within the cage, his feathers slightly ruffled from the recent struggle, his eyes darting between Zunga and the raccoons. The tension in the room was palpable, as if the very air crackled with uncertainty.

The room seemed to crackle with tension as Looney and Moroony responded to Zunga's call. The raccoons entered with a curious mixture of caution and eagerness, their eyes darting between the towering gorilla and the cage-bound canary. "You called, Boss?" Looney inquired, his expression a blend of curiosity and mild amusement.

Zunga's rage was palpable as he pointed towards Rocco with an imperious gesture, his command leaving no room for negotiation. "Take this annoying creature to the dungeon," he ordered, his words laced with venomous irritation.

Rocco, never one to hold his tongue, responded to Zunga's insult with a touch of defiance. "Annoying? Creature? Weren't you the one snoring, like a giant hideous baby, when I was singing? If anyone is annoying, it's you," he retorted, his voice carrying a mix of boldness and exasperation.

The tension in the room escalated as Zunga's anger flared to life, his booming command cutting through the air like a blade.

"NOW!" His voice reverberated, echoing through the chamber with an undeniable force that left no room for hesitation.

Looney and Moroony sprang into action, their movements swift and efficient as they grabbed hold of the cage. With deft coordination, they maneuvered the cage out of the room, closing the door behind them with a soft thud. The canary's defiant retort lingered in the air even as the raccoons departed, a testament to his unyielding spirit.

Once outside the room, Rocco's surroundings shifted as the raccoons carried his cage down the dimly lit corridors of the ship. A sense of unease hung in the air, mingling with Rocco's determination to make the best of the situation. As the cage swung slightly with each step, Rocco seized the opportunity to strike up a conversation, hoping to build a rapport with his captors.

"Hey, you know, I never got the pleasure of knowing your names," Rocco chirped, his tone friendly and inviting. "I'm Rocco."

The raccoons exchanged a glance, a mixture of surprise and uncertainty in their expressions. Moroony spoke up, introducing himself with a friendly tone, "I'm Moroony, and this is my older brother Looney."

However, Looney's response was laced with annoyance as he snapped at his brother. "Shut up, Moroony! Don't talk to him!"

Rocco couldn't help but interject, a playful glint in his eye. "That's not a nice way to talk to your brother, Looney, is it?"

Zunga's furious voice suddenly cut through the air, reminding everyone that he was far from forgotten. "I CAN STILL HEAR

HIM!" His bellow echoed through the corridors, a stark reminder of the gorilla's omnipresence.

Looney's patience seemed to wear thin as he hastily turned to his brother, muttering under his breath, "Let's get out of here before he locks us up in the dungeon."

"Sure, Looney," Moroony agreed, and together they resumed their walk, carrying Rocco's cage between them. Rocco couldn't resist glancing at Moroony, curiosity dancing in his eyes. "Does your brother always boss you around?" he inquired, his tone carrying a hint of understanding.

In the midst of their daring pursuit, Hoppy and Greenie continued their high-speed chase across the water's surface. The wind whistled past them, creating a symphony of rushing air that accompanied their rapid progress. With every bound, Hoppy's legs churned up the water beneath him, leaving a trail of frothy waves in his wake. Greenie held on tightly to Hoppy's shoulder, his eyes scanning the horizon for any sign of the ship they were after.

However, even as their pursuit intensified, Hoppy's stomach began to voice its protests. The rumble of hunger grew louder, a stark reminder that even the most extraordinary feats required sustenance. "I'm getting hungry, Greenie," Hoppy admitted, his words punctuated by a grumble from his belly.

Greenie, always prepared, swiftly produced two juicy apples from Hoppy's pocket. "Don't worry, a couple of apples are on their way!" he reassured, handing them over to his kangaroo companion. Hoppy wasted no time, devouring the apples with a mix of hunger and gratitude.

As the chase continued, time seemed to blur as Hoppy's incredible speed carried them forward. Yet, hunger proved relentless, once again making its presence felt. "Greenie, how many apples do we have left?" Hoppy inquired, his voice tinged with a hint of concern.

"We've got about six left. Why do you ask?" Greenie replied, his curiosity piqued.

"I'm feeling pretty hungry right now. I think I could use a few more," Hoppy admitted, his stomach's demands growing stronger.

Greenie's surprise was palpable; he hadn't anticipated that Hoppy's appetite would resurface so quickly. He distributed a few more apples, his mind racing to calculate their remaining supply against Hoppy's evident hunger.

"Stay positive," Greenie muttered to himself, taking a deep breath to steady his nerves as he continued to provide the kangaroo with apples.

"How much longer?" Hoppy's voice was a mixture of eagerness and impatience, his eyes never leaving the expanse of water ahead.

"The ship should appear any moment now," Greenie assured, his voice filled with anticipation.

But just as Greenie was about to retrieve more apples for Hoppy, the kangaroo's voice cut through his thoughts once again. "Greenie?"

"Yes, Hoppy," Greenie responded, his focus divided.

"I hate to burst your bubble, but those apples, please," Hoppy reminded him, a playful edge in his tone that highlighted his unwavering determination to fulfill his immediate needs.

"Oops, I'm sorry buddy; right this moment," Greenie quickly acknowledged, momentarily sidetracked by the ship's imminent arrival.

The excitement in Greenie's voice was palpable as he pointed out the majestic vessel they had been pursuing. "The Red Carrack!" His exclamation was filled with triumph and eagerness, a testament to the significance of their discovery.

While Hoppy shared in Greenie's exhilaration, he couldn't shake off the persistent hunger that gnawed at his stomach. "Great, but I still need those apples," he reminded Greenie, his resolute determination unwavering even in the face of the impending adventure. "Oh, I'm sorry, I'll get them right away," Greenie replied, his focus shifting back to the task at hand as they closed in on their target.

Amidst the intricate passageways of the Red Carrack, the raccoon brothers Looney and Moroony were on a determined mission. With the canary Rocco confined to his cage, their destination was clear: the ship's dimly lit and foreboding dungeon. The air was tinged with a mixture of tension and determination as they made their way through the ship's narrow corridors.

Inside the cage, Rocco's thoughts churned with a concoction of cunning and desperation. He yearned for his freedom, and he believed he could charm his way out of captivity. In a voice dripping with temptation, he extended an offer that was hard to ignore, "If you release me from this cage, I can fulfill your every desire."

Looney, the stern and wary of the two raccoon brothers, was quick to quash Rocco's proposition. "Be quiet, bird. You've caused so much trouble," he scolded, his frustration evident.

Moroony, on the other hand, displayed a spark of curiosity. "Can you really fetch us anything?" he inquired, his wide eyes betraying his fascination.

"Don't speak to him, Moroony," Looney warned, his tone laced with distrust.

Moroony's response was swift and defiant. "You don't control me," he retorted, refusing to be silenced.

"Yeah, you don't control him," Rocco chimed in from within the confines of his cage, his voice laced with amusement at the brothers' bickering.

Their journey to the ship's dungeon was punctuated by further exchanges. As Moroony's skepticism turned into curiosity, he couldn't resist asking Rocco about his abilities. "Hey bird, you really think you can fetch anything?" he inquired skeptically.

Rocco, unyielding in his charm offensive, retorted confidently, "First of all, my name is Rocco, and yes, I can get whatever you crave. Gold, rubies, pearls, diamonds..."

Moroony's eyes lit up with a simple yet enticing desire, "Can you get us... Potato chips?"

The unexpectedness of Moroony's request caught Rocco off guard for a moment, but he quickly regained his composure. "Potato chips? I can get you a palace full of potato chips," he declared, his voice brimming with confidence.

Moroony, enchanted by the prospect, paused in his steps and exclaimed with childlike excitement, "A palace full of potato chips? Did you hear that, Looney? He's claiming he can provide us with a palace brimming with potato chips."

Looney, never one to indulge in flights of fancy, quickly dismissed the notion with skepticism. "No, he can't!" he retorted, his voice laced with disbelief.

However, Rocco's charm and self-assurance were not easily swayed. "Oh, yes I can," he insisted with a smirk, his confidence unwavering.

Moroony, seemingly won over by Rocco's claims, threw his support behind the canary's audacious assertion. "Oh, yes he can," he affirmed with an excited nod, his imagination ignited by the prospect of a palace filled with potato chips.

On the vast expanse of the open sea, the magnificent Red Carrack dominated the horizon with its grandeur. Greenie's eyes sparkled with admiration as the ship came into full view. "She is absolutely stunning, isn't she?" he remarked, a hint of reverence in his voice.

"Indeed, she is," Hoppy replied, his gaze fixed on the approaching ship. Despite his awe, a sense of concern gnawed at him. "But there's one issue. It's not the ship, it's me. I have no clue where or how to slow down at this speed over water."

Greenie's encouraging voice reassured Hoppy, "Oh. Give it your all and recall how you dashed up the tree with your swiftness; do the same when you make it to the ship and let's keep our fingers crossed."

"Greenie?"

"Yes, Hoppy?"

"Can I have the remaining apples now?" Hoppy inquired, the urgency of his situation apparent in his voice.

Back on the ship, the raccoons continued their animated discussion about Rocco's extravagant promise of a potato chip palace. Moroony's eyes gleamed with excitement as he questioned his brother's skepticism, "How can you be so sure that there isn't a palace brimming with potato chips?"

Looney, practical and grounded, retorted matter-of-factly, "Because the concept of a palace filled with potato chips is simply nonexistent."

Rocco, undeterred by Looney's skepticism, chimed in confidently, his tone dripping with conviction, "Oh, but there is!"

Moroony, swayed by Rocco's certainty, echoed with enthusiasm, "Oh, but there is!"

Exasperated by Moroony's alignment with Rocco's claims, Looney shot back with frustration, "Stop siding with the bird, you fool; he's not telling the truth."

"Are you fibbing, bird?" Moroony inquired of Rocco, seeking clarification.

"I go by Rocco, and FYI, this place is packed with enough chips to take a dip in," Rocco retorted, his confidence unshaken.

"Did you catch that, Looney? You can actually swim in potato chips," Moroony exclaimed, his excitement growing.

Amid the raccoon brothers' fervent argument, Rocco's attention shifted to a fast-approaching figure on the water. "Could it possibly be...?" he wondered silently, his curiosity piqued.

As the two raccoon brothers continued their heated debate, Rocco's eyes remained locked on Hoppy's extraordinary feat of running on water. The canary couldn't contain his amazement. "Unbelievable!" he exclaimed in awe.

"I've already told you, that's impossible!" Looney's voice grew louder in his frustration.

Rocco's focus remained on Hoppy, who showed no sign of slowing down. Concern crept into Rocco's voice, "He's not slowing down. This is going to be a problem."

Moroony, sensing that Rocco was distracted, turned to him and inquired, "Did you say something?"

With his gaze still fixed on Hoppy's remarkable display, Rocco replied, "Yeah, we should start moving before Zunga gets angry again."

"That's the most sensible thing you've said, bird," Looney responded with a hint of grudging respect.

"Yeah, you better hurry up, like right now, before he discovers that we're still here," Rocco warned urgently, his concern for their situation evident.

"We'll discuss this later," Moroony interjected, attempting to pacify the situation.

"Whatever," Looney replied, his frustration evident. Determinedly, the raccoon brothers picked up Rocco's cage and began making their way toward a nearby door on the ship, eager to stay out of Zunga's way.

As the ship drew nearer, its grandeur became more evident to Hoppy. "We'll be on the deck of the vessel soon, just stick to the plan," Greenie reassured him. Hoppy's determination burned brighter with Greenie's words. "I'll give it my all," he replied with conviction.

"Okay, give it your best," Greenie encouraged, his voice a beacon of support.

As the distance between Hoppy and the ship diminished, a surge of panic welled up within him. The ship was even larger up close – a massive structure that towered above him in ways he had never imagined. Hoppy's apprehension got the better of him, and he couldn't help but ask, "Greenie, is it okay to panic?"

"No need to worry. Stay calm and focused. Head to the side of the ship, where it's lowest, and run in a diagonal direction as if the ship was flat," Greenie advised.

"And then what?" Hoppy pressed for more guidance.

"And then we hope for the best," Greenie's voice was unwavering, infused with optimism.

As Hoppy positioned himself closer to the ship's path, he could feel the immense force of the waves it churned up. The waves disrupted his stability, making him fight to keep his balance. With each step, he pushed against the surging water, determined to match the ship's pace.

"Get closer to the ship!" Greenie's voice echoed, urging Hoppy to press on.

"I'm giving it my all," Hoppy's voice was filled with resolve as he poured his energy into the effort.

Soon, Hoppy found himself running parallel to the Red Carrack. He extended his reach towards the ship's side, but the relentless waves were unrelenting, pushing him away. He was tantalizingly close, yet the ship seemed impossibly distant.

"I don't know if I can keep running much longer," Hoppy confessed, his breath coming in ragged gasps.

"Just a little more, don't give up now," Greenie's encouragement resonated in Hoppy's ears, a steady reminder of his unwavering support.

"I'm so exhausted," Hoppy panted, his determination warring with his fatigue as he continued to sprint across the water's surface.

"Try to get as close to the ship as possible. I'll attempt to board it and find something to throw to you," Greenie's voice carried reassurance, a glimmer of hope in the midst of the challenge.

"I won't give up," Hoppy muttered to himself, summoning his inner strength. With a surge of determination, he propelled himself forward, a burst of energy driving him closer to the ship's side. "Just a little closer," Greenie's words were like a lifeline, pulling Hoppy towards his goal.

As Hoppy's leaps brought him closer to the ship, Greenie seized the opportunity to make his move. With a swift, calculated leap, he attached himself to the ship's side, his amphibian agility serving him well as he nimbly climbed his way up to the ship's deck.

"He made it," Hoppy remarked, his voice a mix of awe and anxiety. The sight of Greenie on the ship's deck was both reassuring and daunting, a testament to their teamwork but also a reminder of the distance Hoppy still needed to bridge.

Despite the exhaustion and doubt gnawing at him, Hoppy refused to succumb to them. His eyes remained locked on Greenie's form, determination burning anew. The stakes were high, and he was committed to reaching the ship's side, no matter the challenges that lay ahead.

Bounding onto the ship's deck, Greenie's excitement was palpable as he exclaimed, "Wow, it feels amazing to be back on The Red Carrack!" Without hesitation, he navigated his way towards a familiar spot, his memory guiding his actions. With a sure and agile movement, he scaled onto a suspended lifesaver, ensuring it was firmly secured to its rope. Brimming with determination, Greenie released his grip on the rope that held the lifesaver, causing it to plunge into the water's embrace. With a swift yet calculated motion, he clung onto the lifesaver as it made contact with the water's surface. Swiftly, his mouth found purchase on the rope, and he used his powerful limbs to propel himself through the water, swimming towards Hoppy with remarkable speed.

As Hoppy's weariness threatened to overpower him, a sense of hope ignited within him as the frog closed the distance. The lifesaver was drawing nearer, just within arm's reach. Fueled by a mixture of excitement and exhaustion, he reached out to grab the lifesaver each time it floated tantalizingly close, only for it to slip from his grasp. His stamina waned, and he felt his strength draining. Yet, he refused to give in to the despair that threatened to engulf him. Summoning his remaining energy, Hoppy shouted with newfound determination, "I'm going to leap towards you!"

With an explosion of energy, he propelled himself into the air, defying the weight of fatigue. Simultaneously, Greenie, who had already secured his place on the lifesaver, seized the rope in his mouth and jumped as well. The two of them soared through the air in unison, with Greenie leading the way towards Hoppy's outstretched paw.

In a moment that felt both swift and eternal, Hoppy's paw connected with the rope. He secured his grip with unwavering resolve. However, a powerful wave surged unexpectedly, crashing into Greenie and causing him to lose his hold on the rope. His body was catapulted into the sky, a small figure amidst the vastness.

With reflexes honed by the urgency of the situation, Hoppy extended his free hand, defying the odds to snatch Greenie from the air. The two of them clung to each other as Hoppy's grip on the rope remained unyielding. The force of the wave had sent them into a momentary whirlwind, yet the bond between them proved stronger.

With a surge of determination that bordered on desperation, Hoppy began to pull himself towards the lifesaver. His muscles strained, and his heartbeat seemed to reverberate with the rhythm of his efforts. As he reached the safety of the lifesaver, he carefully placed Greenie onto it, ensuring his friend's well-being above all else.

"That was a close call," Greenie gasped, his voice laced with relief, each breath a testament to their survival after the heart-pounding ordeal. "But we made it!" Hoppy's voice was a mix of exhilaration and exhaustion, his body still recovering from the intense effort and the water he had ingested. "We definitely did."

Greenie's soothing voice broke through the moment, bringing their focus back to their immediate needs. "Greenie, I'm starving," Hoppy confessed, his hunger an undeniable presence in his tone.

"I know you are, buddy," Greenie replied, his reassurance wrapped in empathy as they clung to the lifesaver amidst the vast expanse of the sea.

Chapter Six

The Islands Bell

In the heart of the Red Carrack, hidden away from the ship's bustling activities, lay its dreaded dungeon - a dim and chilling chamber that seemed to emanate an aura of despair. The mischievous raccoons, Looney and Moroony, stood outside the entrance, their expressions a mixture of determination and curiosity. With calculated care, they placed the cage containing Rocco onto the uneven stone floor. The atmosphere was heavy with the knowledge of the bird's captivity, and an air of uncertainty loomed.

Looney stepped forward, his focus intent on the task ahead. He wrestled with a jingling bunch of keys, each one representing a potential route to freedom for the imprisoned canary. As his fingers fumbled through the collection, Rocco's voice, dripping with slyness, cut through the tense silence. "The key you seek lies in the middle, starting from both ends and journeying towards the other end, only to return to the middle." His words carried a playful enigma, an attempt to confound the raccoon's efforts.

Annoyance creased Looney's forehead as he retorted, "Hey, keep it down, bird. I'm trying to focus here!" The irritation in his tone was undeniable, a result of both Rocco's antics and the stress of the situation.

Moroony, meanwhile, held a quieter confidence. Amidst the chaos of unlocking the dungeon door, his focus remained unwavering. "Don't forget to get about the potato chips," Rocco's voice reached his ears in a whisper, a reminder of the quirky bargain they had struck.

"Don't worry, Rocco. I haven't forgotten. It's been on my mind non-stop, and I don't see that changing anytime soon," Moroony reassured him, his determination a reflection of their peculiar yet intriguing exchange.

With a determined twist, Looney finally found the right key. "There!" he exclaimed as the heavy door creaked open, revealing the gloom within. The entrance to the dungeon was a gateway to the unknown, a passage into a realm of shadows.

Rocco's unease was palpable, his gaze fixed on the yawning doorway. "Hey, don't you think it's a bit creepy in there?" His voice wavered slightly, betraying his trepidation.

"Don't worry, Rocco. There's no need to be scared," Moroony's words carried a touch of empathy, an attempt to provide comfort in the face of uncertainty.

With a final exchange of glances, the raccoons hoisted the cage and unceremoniously tossed it into the dungeon's depths. The cage landed on the floor with a heavy thud, its metal bars casting eerie shadows in the dim light. The unsettling silence was broken only by Rocco's voice, his sense of irony prevailing even in the face of captivity. "Hey, was that really necessary?"

"Seriously, how are you still blabbering?" Looney exclaimed.

"With his beak, obviously!" Moroony couldn't resist chiming in, a smirk tugging at his lips.

"I know that, you imbecile! It was a figure of speech," Looney's irritated retort highlighted his dwindling patience as he slammed the door shut and secured it with the key, locking away the canary's protests and presence.

"What a pair of rude individuals!" Rocco's sarcastic comment lingered in the air, a testament to his resilient spirit.

"Yes, they certainly are," a new voice from inside the dungeon answered, hinting at an unexpected twist that would soon unravel. "Hey, who said that?" Rocco's curiosity was piqued, as he found himself in the company of an unexpected fellow prisoner.

Amidst the vast expanse of the ship's deck, Hoppy stood drenched in the aftermath of his daring endeavor. The Red Carrack loomed before him, its grandeur even more imposing up close. The ship's wooden planks creaked underfoot, a reminder of the centuries of maritime history that they bore witness to.

"Whoa, the ship seems even more massive up close," Hoppy marveled, his voice a blend of astonishment and exhaustion. The ship's details, once distant, now captivated his attention – the intricately carved figurehead, the weathered sails billowing in the wind, and the multitude of ropes and rigging that crisscrossed above.

Greenie's practicality cut through the moment of awe. "Let's go find something to eat. I'm sure we can scrounge up some canned food in the storage room," he suggested, the idea of sustenance trumping any lingering sense of wonder.

"I'm so famished, I could devour anything right now," Hoppy admitted with a wry smile, his priorities swiftly shifting from ship admiration to the growling in his stomach. He attempted to dry himself off with a shake, the water droplets glistening in the sunlight before evaporating into the salty air.

The urgency of the situation manifested as approaching voices reached their ears. "Hurry, Hoppy! Jump into one of the barrels!" Greenie's voice held a hint of urgency, propelling Hoppy into swift action. With a quick nod, Hoppy scooped up his amphibian companion and made a snap decision, choosing a barrel from the array that lined the deck. The lid was closed with a soft thud, and they were shrouded in darkness.

Inside the barrel, curiosity danced within Hoppy's mind, mingling with the need for silence. "What are we sitting on in here?" he whispered, his tone a mix of intrigue and puzzlement.

"Shhh, be quiet," Greenie's hushed reply conveyed the urgency of the situation, urging Hoppy to suppress his curiosity for the moment.

As the voices drew nearer, Hoppy's heart pounded in anticipation. The muffled sounds of conversation became clearer, revealing a heated debate unfolding just beyond the confines of the barrel. The ship's deck seemed to hold its breath, as if the very air awaited the outcome of this clandestine exchange.

"Moroony, I've told you countless times, there's no such thing," declared a voice, its tone tinged with exasperation.

"Just because you haven't witnessed it doesn't mean it doesn't exist," Moroony's voice rang out, its unwavering belief in contrast to the skepticism that surrounded him.

"Drop it, Moroony!" another voice interjected, its impatience evident.

Perplexed, Moroony fired back, "Drop what, Looney?"

"Drop the subject, you idiot."

"You're the idiot! Can't you see I am not carrying a subject?"

The exchange painted a picture of the raccoons' ongoing quarrel, their voices echoing with a mix of frustration and humor. Within the barrel, Hoppy's stifled chuckle threatened to escape, a testament to the irony of their situation.

The echoes of the raccoons' quarrel gradually dissolved into the ship's ambiance, leaving behind a sense of lingering tension. Hoppy and Greenie shared a silent understanding, waiting until the coast was clear before daring to move. With cautious precision, they lifted the lid of the barrel, revealing Hoppy's bemused expression as he emerged from his makeshift hiding place. "What exactly was I standing on?" he queried, his voice carrying a blend of confusion and amusement.

Greenie's response carried a sense of concern, "This situation is not ideal."

Curiosity piqued, Hoppy pressed for an explanation, "What do you mean it's not good?"

"Let's find a place to hide before someone spots us. I'll explain everything later," Greenie's tone was urgent, a call to action laced with underlying worry. He jumped onto Hoppy's shoulder, guiding the kangaroo with a sense of purpose. The duo maneuvered through the ship's intricate passages, a blend of excitement and trepidation coursing through their veins.

Their quest led them to a hidden storage unit, a sanctuary amidst the bustling chaos of the ship. Every footstep was deliberate, each movement orchestrated with precision. They slipped into the storage unit, the atmosphere transforming around them. The air grew stagnant and dusty, and the dim light from a solitary window cast long shadows on the stacked crates that surrounded them. The storage room held a sense of forgotten secrecy, a place untouched by the ship's everyday activities.

"Are we really safe here?" Hoppy's voice betrayed his apprehension as they stood within the confined space.

Greenie's reassurance cut through the uncertainty, "Absolutely! Nobody ever comes to this hidden storage. We stashed some extra food here just in case." His words were a balm to Hoppy's anxiety, granting a measure of comfort amidst the unfamiliar environment.

"Move these boxes. We should find a wooden box securely attached to the floor and wall," Greenie directed, his voice a blend of confidence and determination. The boxes were gently shifted aside, the occasional creak of wood against wood serving as a reminder of the ship's age and history.

Amidst the movement, Hoppy's triumphant declaration rang out, "I found it." His hands explored the wooden box, uncovering its hidden treasures. Within its confines lay an array of tin cans, each one labeled with distinct names, evoking a sense of curiosity and mystery.

"Look at this," Hoppy's voice held a mixture of intrigue and excitement. He picked up the first can, reading aloud the words printed on its label: "Creamed Corn."

"Creamed Corn," Greenie couldn't help but chime in, his voice carrying a hint of excitement. "Oh, that's a good one. Find a can opener, and you can give it a try."

As curiosity continued to gnaw at him, Hoppy found himself voicing the question that had been lingering, "How long have these cans been here?" His need to know was driven by a mixture of intrigue and a slight concern for their freshness.

Greenie's response came with a warm smile, alleviating any worry that might have been surfacing. "They have been here for a while, but don't worry; they should still be perfectly fine." His reassurance was like a reassuring hand on Hoppy's shoulder, guiding him through this unexpected culinary adventure.

With determination in his eyes, Hoppy spotted a can opener amidst the storage unit's contents. His excitement surged as he seized the tool, driven by a hunger that had only grown stronger. Skillfully wielding the can opener, he pried open the can of creamy corn with a mix of eagerness and urgency, the metallic scraping sound resonating in the confined space.

The moment the can yielded its contents, Hoppy dove in, hastily devouring the creamy corn. The flavors exploded on his palate, a burst of familiarity mingled with the thrill of newfound discovery. "Mmm, this tastes absolutely amazing," Hoppy's voice was a muffled testament to his delight, his words interwoven with his mouthful of corn.

However, Greenie's response carried a note of concern, interjecting with an air of caution, "Hoppy, this isn't good."

The abrupt halt to Hoppy's indulgence came with a puzzled twist, "But you said it was good!"

Greenie clarified, his voice a mix of seriousness and urgency, "Not the corn, but rather what was hidden inside those barrels."

Perplexed, Hoppy inquired, "Why? They just looked like normal cans, right?"

"Sometimes appearances can be deceiving," Greenie replied cryptically. "Hoppy, savor those retro canned meals for the moment. I need a little while to contemplate."

Before Greenie could even finish his sentence, Hoppy was already reaching for another can, his insatiable hunger driving him forward with an almost single-minded determination.

Meanwhile, in the depths of the ship's dungeon, the atmosphere was heavy with intrigue and anticipation. Rocco had finished recounting his tale, every word carrying the weight of his determination to unravel the mysteries that surrounded him. With a newfound sense of courage, he found his voice, demanding the presence of the enigmatic figure that had been lurking in the shadows.

A melodic yet skeptical female voice emanated from a concealed corner, as if testing the veracity of Rocco's narrative. "Is that really your story?" Her tone carried a hint of doubt, her words like a cautious dance in the darkness.

Rocco stood firm, unswayed by her skepticism. His response held the conviction of someone who had entered into a binding agreement. "Yes, it is indeed my story. We made a deal, and now it's your turn to reveal yourself." His words rang out in the dimly lit chamber, a challenge thrown into the void.

The tension within the dungeon seemed to intensify, the air thick with the anticipation of the hidden figure's response. Seconds felt like minutes as the weight of their exchange hung in the air.

And then, a voice, calm and steady, began to weave a captivating tale of its own. "Allow me to clarify the captivating tale. You were a courageous prince, leading an army of majestic birds on a covert mission. However, your noble mission takes a dangerous turn when you find yourself under attack by colossal falcons." The voice wove a narrative that danced between reality and fantasy, drawing the listeners into its web of intrigue.

"Astonishingly, you emerge as the sole survivor on both sides of the confrontation. But let it be known that you didn't flee from the battle; instead, you valiantly vanquished each falcon that dared to stand against you." The voice painted a picture of valor and triumph, of a prince who refused to back down even in the face of overwhelming odds.

The tale continued to unfold, weaving a tapestry of a life filled with challenges and choices. "Following these awe-inspiring events, you made a life-altering decision to settle down. Embracing a new chapter in your life, you established a family and relished in the joys of being the esteemed ruler of the bird kingdom." The story took unexpected turns, adding layers of complexity to the prince's character.

"Ten years had passed since the falcons sought to wreak havoc. They resorted to kidnapping individuals from your community, and now you find yourself volunteering for their release and Zunga has taken on the task of delivering you to the falcon boss." The voice's words echoed through the dungeon, each sentence like a brushstroke on the canvas of Rocco's fate.

The voice paused, as if allowing the gravity of the tale to sink in. "Did I miss anything?" The question hung in the air, waiting for acknowledgment. Rocco nodded, his response carrying a blend of affirmation and determination. "There is more, but you get the idea," he said, his voice unwavering.

"You are a funny little thing," the voice remarked, its tone carrying a mixture of amusement and curiosity. Rocco, refusing to be labeled as an object, quickly retorted, "I'm not a thing. My name is Rocco. Now, who are you?" His determination to establish his identity was palpable.

With an air of intrigue, the voice responded, "I apologize. It's a pleasure to make your acquaintance, Rocco. My name is Kitteli," the voice emerged from the depths of darkness, revealing itself as a being with its own consciousness. "However, in most circles, I am known as Zatara," she continued, her voice gaining an air of mystery. As the shadows receded, an aged black rat with long silver hair and a white tail adorned with chains stepped forward, her presence commanding attention.

Rocco's eyes widened in disbelief as he uttered the name, "The witch Zatara?" The legend he had heard about was unfolding before him.

With a hint of amusement in her voice, Zatara confirmed, "That would be me." Her aura exuded a sense of ancient wisdom, and the chains adorning her added an aura of mystique.

Rocco's astonishment was evident as he couldn't help but exclaim, "No way?" The encounter was beyond anything he could have imagined.

Feeling the urgency of their situation, Rocco pleaded, "Can you help me get out of this cage?" His voice carried a mix of hope and desperation, his small form confined within the limits of his prison.

Zatara's voice held a touch of regret as she replied, "I am sorry, I'm afraid these chains won't let me get that far." Her vulnerability was palpable, hinting at a deeper layer to her story.

"How long have you been stuck here?" Rocco inquired, his curiosity fueled by compassion for the enigmatic figure before him.

"It's been about three months since I've been confined on this ship," Zatara revealed, her voice carrying the weight of her imprisonment. "The raccoons only bring me enough food and water to survive. Zunga wants to keep me alive, but he enjoys keeping me weak, otherwise, I would have perished a long time ago." Her words painted a grim picture of her predicament.

Rocco's curiosity was unwavering as he probed further, "What about you? Why does Zunga have an interest in you? How did you end up in this situation? And this time, tell the truth," Zatara's own inquiry demanded transparency.

"I suppose Zunga found me interesting. Here's the real story of how I got here," Rocco replied, honesty lacing his words as he recounted his tale. However, he carefully omitted any mention of

Hoppy and Greenie, knowing that their connection could change the dynamics of the conversation.

After Rocco finished recounting his story, he couldn't help but express his concern about their destination, "Where are they transporting us?"

"We are en route to the Central Banking Island, which has been seized by pirates," Zatara responded, her voice tinged with a mixture of worry and uncertainty.

"I heard about the pirates taking over the island. Is history going to repeat itself?" Rocco's voice carried a sense of unease, the implications of their destination not lost on him.

Zatara's response was laced with a similar worry, "Let's just hope nothing evil happens."

As their conversation continued, a distant sound of bells resonated through the air, catching Rocco's attention. "What's that noise? A bell?" he questioned, his curiosity piqued once again.

"We'll reach the island in a little while," Zatara announced, her tone indicating that their destination was drawing near. She turned to Rocco, her eyes locking onto his with a sense of urgency. "Rocco, I need your help. Can I rely on you?"

Rocco's determination was unwavering as he replied, "You can count on me! What do you need me to do?"

"The raccoons will be arriving soon," Zatara warned, her voice steady but urgent. "Looks like Zunga wants a new companion."

"I'm not anyone's companion," Rocco declared firmly, his voice carrying a sense of independence and defiance.

"Alright, you're not anyone's companion. Listen carefully; Zunga will not set me free until the appropriate moment. If you are able to escape, I need you to locate Lagartha, a lizard bartender. She has allies, and you need to inform her of my current situation. Also, make sure to reassure her that my sisters are currently safe. They need to reach them before the pirates do," Zatara's voice held a mix of desperation and determination.

Rocco's determination remained resolute as he inquired, "Where are your sisters hiding, and where can I locate Lagartha?" The weight of their mission hung in the air, their destinies intertwined in ways they could never have foreseen.

In the dimly lit storage room, Hoppy found a comfortable spot to rest, his body finally succumbing to a much-needed nap after sating his hunger with the canned food. The sensation of his stomach no longer gnawing at him brought a sense of relief that allowed him to relax. His eyes drooped as he settled into a makeshift nest among the boxes, the room's ambiance cocooning him in a hushed tranquility.

Meanwhile, Greenie perched thoughtfully on a nearby crate, his gaze distant as he grappled with the weight of their circumstances. His contemplations swirled like the currents of the ocean, tracing back to the moment their adventure had taken an unexpected turn. The mysteries that unfolded and the alliances forged were now part of their reality, and Greenie couldn't help but wonder how they had arrived at this crossroads.

Amid his introspection, a subtle sound resonated in the air, breaking through the silence like a gentle ripple on the water's surface. "The Islands Bell! I can hear it," Greenie's voice carried a mixture of surprise and urgency. The revelation snapped him out of his reverie, his eyes widening with realization. He knew what this sound meant – their journey was nearing its next chapter.

"Hoppy, wake up!" Greenie's voice rang out with an energy that betrayed the calm atmosphere of the storage room. His words were a gentle yet urgent call, a reminder that their time for rest was coming to an end. The impending arrival at their destination demanded their attention, and Greenie's excitement was palpable.

With a yawn and a stretch, Hoppy roused from his slumber, blinking his eyes open. The nap had brought a renewed vitality, and he could sense the anticipation in Greenie's voice. Pushing himself to his feet, he met Greenie's gaze and absorbed the urgency that radiated from his friend's expression.

"We're almost there," Greenie declared, his words carrying the weight of their impending encounter with fate. The Islands Bell's chime had marked a turning point in their journey, signaling the approach of Central Banking Island and the uncertain challenges that awaited them there. The air felt charged with anticipation, and Hoppy's heart raced with a mixture of excitement and apprehension.

Chapter Seven

Concealed Beneath The Hat

The atmosphere onboard the ship was charged with anticipation as the vessel gradually slowed its pace, its massive form coming to a graceful halt as it neared the bustling docks of Central Banking Island. The creaking of the ship's timbers and the gentle lapping of water against its sides created a symphony of sounds that signaled their arrival. Greenie stood at the ready, his keen senses attuned to the environment around them.

Greenie's voice was filled with a mix of certainty and contemplation as he remarked, "I've finally arrived. Nothing happens by chance." His words held a sense of purpose, as if he believed that destiny had guided them to this point. The adventure they had embarked upon seemed to have an underlying logic that was yet to be fully unraveled.

"What do you mean?" Hoppy's curiosity was evident in his voice, his inquisitive nature pushing him to seek a deeper understanding.

Greenie's gaze met Hoppy's as he explained, "If it hadn't been for you and that bothersome bird, it would have taken me an eternity to reach this place. There must be a logical reason behind all this." His conviction was unwavering, a testament to his belief in the interconnectedness of events.

"I'm grateful that our paths crossed as well," Hoppy replied with a warm smile, acknowledging the bond that had formed between them in the midst of their shared challenges.

As they stood within the storage room, the ship's vibrations seemed to echo the rhythm of their hearts. Hoppy's curiosity led him to inquire about their next steps. "What should we do next?" he asked, eager to embark on the next phase of their journey.

Greenie's response was measured and composed, "We wait. Someone will secure the ship to the dock. Once it's safe, we'll disembark and search for a lizard who works as a bartender on the island." His words held a sense of strategy, a plan unfolding amidst the uncertainty of their surroundings.

Outside the storage room, the world was in motion. Muffled sounds filtered through, offering a glimpse into the activities taking place. The echo of footsteps and hushed conversations painted a picture of purposeful movements, a sense of preparation for a significant event.

Greenie's voice broke through the ambient sounds as he noted, "It won't be long until the ship is cleared." His optimism was palpable, a beacon of hope that radiated within the confined space.

As they awaited the next developments, they overheard the distinct noise of the ship's dock being lowered, marking the progression of their journey. The synchronized movements of the crew and the orchestrated sounds of the ship coming to rest against the dock added to the sense of impending change.

Meanwhile, on the ship's deck, Zunga's authoritative presence was felt as he prepared to disembark. His command to the raccoons to retrieve the canary was a clear indication of his intentions. Inside the dungeon, Rocco and Zatara were well aware of the approaching raccoons. Zatara, bound by chains but not devoid of determination, spoke with a serene wisdom, "I believe they've come to retrieve you, my friend."

The jingling of keys and the creaking of the dungeon door being unlocked marked the impending moment of their meeting. As the door swung open, Looney's silhouette was framed against the light, a figure that stood between the confined canary and the unknown beyond.

"It's time to go, Bird!" Looney declared, his voice carrying a mixture of authority and impatience. Rocco, though confined in a cage, asserted his identity with determination, "My name is Rocco!" His words held a spark of defiance, a reminder that he was not just a captive but an individual with his own sense of self.

With the raccoon brothers at the helm, Rocco's cage was carried towards the ship's deck, setting the stage for their next phase of adventure. As they emerged into the open air, Rocco's eyes widened at the sight that greeted him. The docks of Central Banking Island were a hub of frenetic activity, a bustling canvas painted with the vibrant colors of numerous pirate ships. Each ship, adorned with its own distinctive flag, stood as a testament to the diverse array of crews that had converged upon this enigmatic island. The air was thick with the mingling scents of saltwater, wooden planks, and the promise of adventure.

Rocco's voice cut through the ambient sounds as he voiced his genuine curiosity, "What are all these ships doing here?" The question hung in the air, revealing the wonderment that the sight before him had evoked. The multitude of vessels, ranging from massive galleons to agile schooners, was a spectacle that beckoned exploration.

Moroony, one of the raccoon brothers, provided an answer with a matter-of-fact tone, "They are unloading their goods." His words hinted at the island's role as a trading hub, a place where pirates from across the seas converged to exchange their treasures.

Rocco's thirst for knowledge persisted as he sought further understanding, "And then?" The anticipation in his voice was palpable, a desire to unravel the sequence of events that unfolded on this bustling stage.

"After that, they take it to the Central Banking building," Moroony explained. His response painted a clearer picture of the island's functioning, implying that the treasures exchanged on the docks found their way to the heart of Central Banking Island.

Rocco's mind whirred with curiosity, prompting him to pose yet another question, "How can there be so many pirate ships? Are they all unloading stolen goods?" His inquiry peeled back the layers of intrigue, shedding light on the potential origins of the treasures that were being unloaded.

Before Moroony could respond, his brother interjected with a note of urgency, directing their attention elsewhere. "Hey, Moroony, be quiet! Zunga is on his way." The raccoon brothers' hushed exchange was a reminder of the tension that lingered, the constant vigilance required in the presence of their imposing leader.

Zunga's arrival onto the ship's deck was marked by a sense of authority. His presence exuded power, and in his hands, he held a medium-sized chest that hinted at secrets waiting to be unveiled. The raccoon brothers and Rocco stood poised, a scene that underscored their readiness to comply with his commands.

Rocco's mischievous spirit couldn't be suppressed as he greeted Zunga, "Hey, Zunga buddy, did you miss me?" His words, laced with a touch of playfulness, juxtaposed against the stern atmosphere that surrounded them.

Zunga's impatience was palpable as he snapped at the raccoons, his words commanding their obedience, "Give me that cage, you idiots, and take this chest to the Central building!" His words brooked no argument, a reminder of his authority in this domain.

Amidst the interaction, Rocco's curiosity was piqued once more. "Ooh, what's inside the chest? Could it be meant for me?" His eagerness was undeniable, a manifestation of his unyielding spirit of inquiry.

Zunga's response was swift and harsh, "Quiet, bird! If you don't stop making noise, I'll toss you into the chest." His words held a threat that silenced Rocco momentarily.

However, Rocco's wit remained intact, and he replied, "In that case, I'll finally get to discover what's hidden within." His words, a playful retort, hinted at his tenacious resolve to uncover the truth.

But Zunga's patience was at its limit as he shouted, "Be quiet!" The force in his voice was a clear directive that demanded obedience.

With a tone of mock submission, Rocco responded, "Alright, alright, no need to yell. I'll stay silent until something interesting catches my eye." His words held a promise tinged with humor, a hint that his insatiable curiosity might yet be contained, at least for the moment.

The ship's deck breathed a sigh of relief as Zunga disembarked, the raccoons under his command dutifully following with the chest in tow. The wooden platform echoed with the rhythm of their footsteps, each one a testament to the solemn procession taking place. As they traversed the platform, Zunga's stern gaze shifted towards Rocco, a question poised on his lips, "Did the rat say anything?"

Rocco's response carried a trace of sarcasm, "Oh, now you want me to talk?" His words dripped with playful defiance, a reminder of the dynamics between them.

"Talk, bird!" Zunga's demand was sharp, revealing his impatience.

Rocco's retort held a hint of nonchalance, "Um, sorry, could you repeat the question? I wasn't really listening." His words played into the ongoing banter, a game they both seemed accustomed to.

The frustration in Zunga's voice was palpable as he reiterated, "I asked if the rat said anything."

Rocco's casual tone persisted, "Rat? What rat? I absolutely despise rats." His words danced on the edge of jest, hinting at the elaborate tale he was weaving.

The exasperation in Zunga's voice grew as he probed further, "You mean to tell me you didn't spot a rat in the dungeon?"

114

Rocco's response was swift, "Not at all. The rat must have gotten frightened when those Raccoons tossed me into the dungeon. I remember saying, 'I hope there aren't any rats in here! I can't stand them! Why?'"

Zunga's dismissal was curt, "Forget about it." His words cut through the exchange, indicating his readiness to move on.

As the scene unfolded, Rocco's observant eyes took in the flurry of activity around him. Pirates and their attendants disembarked from their ships, a display of varied characters contributing to the vibrant tableau. Among them, a towering tiger emerged, drawing Rocco's attention like a magnet.

Unable to suppress his curiosity, Rocco voiced his question, "Who's that colossal tiger?" His words were tinged with awe, a reflection of the imposing presence the tiger commanded.

Zunga's response was tinged with irritation, "Quit talking, bird!" His words were a reminder of the unspoken rule that Rocco's inquiries were not welcome.

Rocco's patience waned, his retort sharp, "Here we go again with the 'shut up'." His words held a note of exasperation, a testament to his determination to engage in conversation.

In the midst of this exchange, Zunga and the tiger found themselves in a confrontation of their own, their eyes locking in an intense stare-down. The imposing tiger, Trigger, held a mischievous grin on his face as he addressed Zunga, "I heard you arrived." His words were laced with a subtle hint of jest, a testament to the familiarity they shared.

Zunga's response was terse, "Trigger."

The tiger's curiosity was unquenched as he gestured towards the cage Zunga held, "What do you have there?"

Zunga's sly smile held a touch of amusement, "This is my pet bird." His words were enigmatic, hinting at a deeper narrative.

Rocco's voice cut through the exchange from within his cage, his declaration defiant, "I am no one's pet, and my name is Rocco!" The fire in his words matched the fiery spirit that defined him, a canary unyielding in the face of adversity.

Trigger's presence exuded an undeniable aura of intimidation, a testament to his fearsome reputation. His voice carried a weight of experience as he commented, "I see you found a feisty one," his eyes fixed on Rocco, a mixture of intrigue and calculation dancing in their depths. Rocco's response was marked by an unwavering determination, his gaze unwaveringly meeting the tiger's, a silent challenge issued.

Zunga, determined to assert his authority, boasted confidently, "I'll teach him manners." His words held a note of pride, as if the task of taming the rebellious canary was a personal conquest.

Trigger's eyes gleamed with mischief, an impish grin playing on his lips as he contemplated Rocco's defiance. "I'll trade you with my pet," he proposed, his tone suggestive of a playful wager. His gaze remained locked on the canary, curious about the depths of the bird's spirit.

Rocco's response was unwavering, his defiance a steadfast pillar that defined him. "How about I teach you both manners?" His words were laden with a challenge, a declaration of his indomitable spirit that dared to stand up against the odds.

Laughter erupted from both Zunga and Trigger, a chorus of dismissive amusement that underestimated Rocco's audaciousness. In that moment, Rocco stood as a symbol of resilience, refusing to be belittled or subdued.

Trigger's voice broke through the mirth, a tone of seriousness replacing the laughter. "Hey, Zunga, we need to have a conversation."

Zunga's response was a display of prioritization, "I'll catch up with you later. I must take this chest to the Central building first." His words were a reminder of the tasks that occupied his immediate attention.

Trigger's curiosity was insatiable as he prodded further, "Is that it?" His inquisitive nature seemed to harbor a deeper interest.

Zunga's confirmation was succinct, "It is." His tone carried a note of finality, suggesting that this topic was not open for further discussion.

Trigger's agreement was casual, "Alright, I'll catch you later then." His words were a promise, a nod to the camaraderie they shared.

The conversation flowed seamlessly, seamlessly transitioning to another topic. Trigger's voice held a hint of intrigue as he inquired, "By the way, any progress in locating them?" His words danced on the edge of secrecy, revealing that they were discussing matters of importance.

Zunga's response was affirmative, "We've got a lead." The assurance in his tone hinted at a plan in motion, a sign of progress.

Trigger's approval was palpable, "Great." His words carried a note of satisfaction, an acknowledgment of a job well done.

The conversation concluded with Trigger's curiosity leading the way, "Where's Chango?" His question lingered in the air, a thread of curiosity waiting to be woven.

Zunga's answer was swift, "He's on a mission." His words carried an air of mystery, suggesting that Chango was engaged in significant undertakings.

Rocco, eager to glean some information from the cryptic conversation, squawked inquisitively, "What are you guys discussing? Can someone fill me in?" His words held a blend of urgency and curiosity.

In a thrilling moment of suspense, the ship's environment became enveloped in a palpable silence, heightening the tension that surrounded our protagonists. The stillness seemed to hold its breath, as if the vessel itself was bracing for what would come next.

From their vantage point within the hidden storage room, Greenie's voice emerged as a whisper, barely audible, "There's no sound or movement coming from the vessel."

"Perfect," Hoppy responded in a hushed tone, his curiosity and caution guiding his next steps. He rose to his feet, his eyes fixed on the door that separated him from the outside world.

A note of practicality entered Greenie's voice as he intervened, "Hold on, Hoppy. You can't go outside looking like that. The last thing we want is for the pirates to spot a walking Kangaroo. It's been quite some time since I last set foot in this place. We always used to stash spare clothes here. There must be a bunch of old garments tucked away somewhere. Help me in searching for them; we need to conceal your identity."

Guided by Greenie's suggestion, Hoppy grabbed a couple of boxes and began the process of discovery. The first box opened to reveal an unexpected collection of chemical supplies, each bottle stamped with the image of a plant. Hoppy's voice resonated with awe, "Wow, I found some chemical supplies with a plant stamped on the bottles!"

Beside him, Greenie's tone held a touch of disbelief, "Those are still around?"

Undeterred, Hoppy moved on to the next box, unveiling a collection of lab tubes. Holding one up for Greenie to see, he shared his discovery. Greenie's curiosity was quick to emerge, "Are any broken?"

Hoppy's response was upbeat, "Not at all, they're in perfect condition."

Greenie's chuckle held a sense of nostalgia, "They don't make them like they used to."

With a renewed sense of anticipation, Hoppy opened the third box, revealing its enigmatic contents. A black round hat, seemingly mundane yet tinged with a touch of mystery, lay within. Pulling it out, Hoppy's excitement became palpable as he turned to Greenie, "This looks promising."

Greenie's response was a mix of recognition and fondness, "That's Mr. Jenkins' hat!"

Eager to embrace the transformative power of the hat, Hoppy followed Greenie's advice, placing it on his head. The sense of concealment and intrigue was immediate, as the hat's brim worked its magic in masking his distinct kangaroo ears.

Driven by curiosity and a desire to immerse himself in this newfound identity, Hoppy decided to delve further into the stash of clothes. Emptying the box onto the floor, he was met with an array of neatly pressed garments, each holding its own story.

Among the assortment, one item captured Hoppy's attention – a white button-up shirt with long sleeves. Carefully selecting it from the pile, he shed the shirt and vest that had been his companions since his journey began. The transition felt symbolic, as if he was shedding his old self and embracing a new persona. With a mix of anticipation and a hint of unease, Hoppy donned the white shirt, meticulously fastening each button. The fabric felt unfamiliar against his skin, and the scent of memories long forgotten wafted from its fibers.

Greenie's inquisitiveness took the form of a question, "How does it feel?"

After a moment of thoughtful consideration, Hoppy responded, "It's a bit big and smells a bit odd, but other than that, it's alright."

Amidst the assortment of clothes, Hoppy's eyes fell upon a sleek black jacket, its presence exuding an air of mystery and sophistication. He carefully lifted it, allowing his fingers to trace the contours of its fabric. The jacket's oversized nature was apparent, its length and sleeves extending beyond the ordinary. As he donned the jacket, it transformed him, almost resembling a coat that engulfed him in its embrace. Determination sparked in his eyes as he rolled up the sleeves, adjusted the fit, and lifted the collar with a sense of flair. Seeking validation, he couldn't resist asking, "So, what's the verdict?"

Greenie's voice was a mix of recognition and amusement, "I totally recognize that jacket."

Hoppy's spirits soared as he affirmed, "It feels incredible." The oversized jacket, despite its unconventional fit, seemed to infuse him with a newfound confidence.

Greenie's smile mirrored his sentiments, "Great pick! It really enhances the whole outfit. Now, let's disembark from the ship and see if we can uncover some cherished memories."

With Greenie's characteristic agility and mischievous spirit, he effortlessly leaped onto Hoppy's shoulder, his small paws barely making a sound against the fabric. In a swift, fluid motion, he delicately lifted the hat that rested on Hoppy's head and slipped within its depths, disappearing from sight.

"Let's go," Greenie declared, the palpable excitement in his tone evident even in his hushed voice.

"Ouch! Keep your voice down," Hoppy winced, his long kangaroo ears twitching with sensitivity. "You're literally talking in my ear."

"Sorry," Greenie whispered, his words barely audible, a testament to their need for stealth.

As Hoppy and Greenie disembarked from the ship, the bustling activity of the dock unfurled before them. The sight was a dynamic symphony of movement, as pirates and their servants worked tirelessly to unload the stolen goods that their ships bore. The dock had transformed into a hub of organized chaos, each pirate ship contributing to the growing pile of ill-gotten treasures.

Hoppy's voice carried a touch of awe and surprise, "I did not know there were this many pirates before."

The dock painted a vivid picture of piratical activity, with pirates engaged in various tasks. The scene, a blend of intrigue and unease, made Hoppy's heart race in anticipation of the unknown that lay ahead.

Navigating through the bustling dock, Hoppy and Greenie became inadvertent eavesdroppers to the pirates' conversations. The air buzzed with the clinking of gold, the raucous laughter of triumphant pirates, and the occasional heated exchange. The atmosphere was electric, charged with the energy of pirates reveling in their gains. It was a sight that defied Hoppy's expectations, and he found himself immersed in a world he had only heard about in stories.

Hippos moved with surprising agility, carrying crates laden with stolen treasures. Monkeys swung from ropes, acting as the diligent organizers of the amassed loot. Mighty elephants, their strength evident, took on the responsibility of transporting the heavier cargo, while parrots occupied strategic perches, barking orders to ensure the efficient functioning of the operations.

Greenie's voice offered guidance, a whisper of caution, "Watch your step and be mindful of others around you. Inexperienced individuals are always looking for trouble."

Curious about their next steps, Hoppy inquired, "Where to now?"

Greenie shared the path with a clear sense of direction, "Once you reach the end of the dock, make a left turn. Ahead, the path will split. Take the leftward trail, leading you uphill. From there, you'll gain a clear vantage point of the island's downtown area."

Amidst the whirlwind of activity, Hoppy's curiosity found its focus on the question of what would become of the stolen goods. His inquisitive nature took over, prompting him to inquire of Greenie, "Where are all these stolen goods being transported to?"

Greenie's response held the assurance of knowledge, "The stolen goods are collected from various lands. They are being taken to the Central Banking Building."

Puzzled by the purpose, Hoppy pressed on, "But why? What's the reason behind gathering them all there?"

Greenie paused, contemplating the complexity of the situation, before offering his insight, "There are many reasons behind it. However, for now, our main goal is to reach our destination."

Continuing their journey, Hoppy's excitement grew as the downtown area gradually came into view. His exclamation was brimming with enthusiasm, "Look, Greenie! The hill has brought us to the perfect vantage point. Downtown is already visible!"

Concealed beneath the hat, Greenie's eyes sparkled with a sense of wonder as he peered out at the unfolding panorama. His delight was palpable as he exclaimed, "What a breathtaking view! It never ceases to amaze!"

Hoppy nodded, his own amazement mirrored in his expression. "Absolutely, it's truly splendid," he agreed. As they stood together, Greenie began to share the story behind the magnificent downtown before them.

"This awe-inspiring creation," Greenie began, his voice tinged with a mix of admiration and respect, "was brought to life by the dedication of countless animals, each driven by a single purpose."

Hoppy's gaze roved over the remarkable architectural feat, his eyes tracing the lines of the stunning buildings that painted the skyline. The view from their hilltop vantage point was nothing short of breathtaking. It was evident that whoever had orchestrated this impressive work had poured their heart and soul into its realization.

Their journey continued as Hoppy took step after step, his feet leading them through the bustling streets until they arrived at the very heart of the city.

With genuine curiosity, Hoppy inquired, "What should I do now?"

Greenie's guidance was clear and confident, "You'll find the bar just around the corner on your left. There are a number of options along that block. Look for the one with a bold sign that reads, 'Bad Boys drink here! No Fear!'"

Following Greenie's guidance, Hoppy's eyes wandered to the left. His gaze swept across the vibrant street, a hub of activity with a variety of lively bars. With a resolute stride, he set forth on his next adventure, drawn to the convergence of excitement that lay ahead. Crossing the street to the other side, he was met with a dazzling array of signs adorning the front of each establishment.

And then, like a beacon of intrigue, one sign caught his eye, its bold letters demanding attention against the cityscape. In confident proclamation, the sign declared, "Bad boys drink here. No fear!" The words resonated with an air of rebellion, adventure, and the promise of something out of the ordinary.

Navigating through the bustling street, Hoppy's steps were accompanied by Greenie's presence hidden beneath his hat. Caution was their watchword as they threaded their way through the throng of creatures that populated the area. The sheer diversity of beings present was a testament to the island's magnetism, drawing in fierce animals and formidable pirates alike. A tangible excitement hung in the air, tinged with an undercurrent of potential danger.

As they neared the bar, Hoppy's gaze was fixed on the aged structure that loomed before them. It carried an air of history and a hint of intimidation. The worn wood and the slightly crooked sign swinging overhead seemed to tell stories of countless visitors who had crossed its threshold. The scent of mustiness pervaded the surroundings, adding to the atmosphere that enveloped the place.

With resolute determination, Hoppy mounted the two steps that led up to the bar's porch. The creak of the wood beneath his weight seemed to echo in the quiet corners of his mind, reminding him of the countless stories that had unfolded within these walls.

Standing at the threshold, his hand reaching for the door, Hoppy leaned closer to Greenie and whispered, "Okay, I'm about to enter the bar. Hey, hold on a second."

Perplexed, Greenie responded in hushed tones, "What's the matter?"

Hoppy's finger pointed discreetly toward a wall adorned with posters. "Look," he directed, his tone a mixture of surprise and intrigue.

Following Hoppy's line of sight, Greenie's eyes widened as he saw multiple posters with his own picture on them. "What?" he exclaimed, his voice barely above a whisper.

Nodding, Hoppy confirmed, "Yeah, they're all over the entrance and a few on the walls. Actually, they're quite stylish, like some sort of cool wanted poster."

"Wanted?" Greenie echoed, disbelief coloring his voice.

"Yep," Hoppy affirmed, "and it says 'Frog Wanted Alive' right there."

Greenie's incredulity deepened as he inquired, "Alive? Seriously?"

Hoppy's lips quirked into a small smile as he added, "And guess what, Greenie? The reward's a hundred thousand golden coins."

Greenie's reaction was swift and indignant, "Only a hundred thousand? What a bunch of cheapskates!"

Chapter Eight

Is He Here?

Just as Hoppy was poised to cross the threshold into the rustic, time-worn bar, a storming force suddenly emerged, propelling him aside with all the gentleness of a tempestuous gale. A furious rhino, all pent-up energy and brimming hostility, had charged out of the bar, barely sparing Hoppy a second glance in his path.

Taken aback by the abrupt shove, Hoppy muttered indignantly under his breath, "No manners," his voice layered with disbelief at the blatant lack of consideration displayed by the rhino. The sheer audacity of the encounter lingered in his mind, leaving him astounded by the rhino's audacious behavior.

Unbeknownst to Hoppy, his muttered remark had not escaped the rhino's attention. The colossal figure of the rhino pivoted on his hooves, fixing his fierce gaze upon Hoppy. His brow furrowed, a mixture of anger and curiosity brimming in his deep-set eyes. In a rumbling voice that matched his imposing demeanor, he grumbled, "You say something?"

Caught off guard, Hoppy's heart raced for a moment, but he quickly regained his composure. Realizing that engaging in a conversation with the rhino could potentially escalate matters, he wisely opted for discretion. With a quick shake of his head, he muttered a soft, "No, sir."

However, Greenie, hidden beneath Hoppy's hat, had other plans. Urging Hoppy on, he whispered insistently, "Apologize right away!"

Sighing inwardly, Hoppy knew it was best to diffuse the situation. "I'm sorry, sir," he offered, his voice carrying a tone of contrition.

But the rhino was not satisfied. "I didn't hear you," he bellowed, his demeanor unrelenting.

Greenie's voice continued to echo, "Say it louder, say it louder..."

Summoning a bit more courage, Hoppy repeated with a touch more volume, "I apologize, sir."

"Once more!" the rhino demanded, his sheer presence commanding attention.

"One more time, one more time..." Greenie's insistence persisted.

Sighing audibly this time, Hoppy complied, "I apologize, sir," his tone a blend of earnestness and apology.

The rhino's gaze bore into Hoppy, his warning clear, "You better pray I don't bump into you again!" With a final, menacing glance, the rhino pivoted on his massive form, resuming his path with determined strides. Every step reverberated through the ground, leaving behind a palpable sense of unease in his wake.

As the rhino's figure gradually diminished in the distance, Hoppy let out a sigh of relief, allowing his tense shoulders to finally relax. "I thought he would never leave," he muttered, a mixture of exasperation and relief coursing through his words. "Those few seconds were intense."

"Stay quiet, Hoppy, unless I give you permission to speak," Greenie's voice issued a cautionary reminder. "Don't start imitating Rocco's behavior. If the Pirates discover that I'm concealed under your hat, they would tear me apart into countless pieces."

Hoppy's determination flared, his gaze unwavering as he stepped through the saloon-style doors, ushering himself into the heart of the dimly lit bar. The very air seemed to pulse with a unique blend of excitement and danger. Groups of rough-edged animals occupied the space, their tattered attire and battle-hardened demeanors speaking volumes of their countless escapades and fierce confrontations.

The atmosphere was a cacophony of laughter and boisterous chatter, intertwining with the symphony of clinking tankards and the rhythmic shuffling of cards on tabletops. The room was alive with a charged energy, a medley of camaraderie and rivalry that coexisted in an uneasy yet undeniable harmony.

In the midst of this vibrant chaos, Hoppy's senses were on full alert, his eyes capturing the spectacle of pirates exchanging tales of perilous journeys and bands of rogues regaling one another with accounts of their latest daring feats. It was an environment unlike any he had encountered, and he experienced a cocktail of emotions—awe, curiosity, and a twinge of anxiety—as he prepared to navigate the labyrinthine personalities that thrived in such a tumultuous setting.

"Do you see a bartender?" Greenie's voice, a subtle whisper, emanated from the depths beneath the concealing hat.

Squinting through the haze, Hoppy's gaze landed upon a figure gliding through the crowd on roller skates, a tray of drinks in her deft hands. "I see a lizard carrying a tray... roll skating our way?" he responded, his eyes wide in amazement.

A chuckle resonated from the unseen frog. "It's not her," Greenie's tone was laced with a sense of certainty, as if he had already unraveled the riddle.

Piqued by Greenie's conviction, Hoppy couldn't help but ask, "How did you know it's not her without visual confirmation?"

There was a beat of silence, a pause that seemed to hang in the air before Greenie's response unfurled. "Look around you and tell me how many lizards on roller-skates with trays do you see?"

Following Greenie's prompt, Hoppy's gaze swept across the bustling scene. He soon identified a contingent of eight female lizard waitstaff, each a vision of agility and poise as they gracefully maneuvered on their roller skates. Their petite frames belied their astonishing speed and precision, allowing them to navigate the crowded space with a seamless grace that drew the eye.

Spellbound, Hoppy's gaze tracked their movements, captivated by their intricate ballet. As if in a carefully choreographed performance, a couple of the lizards launched themselves into acrobatic spins and flips, their trays a natural extension of their lithe forms. The trays glided through the air like partners in an intricate dance, untouched by the laws of gravity, a testament to their remarkable skill and finesse.

In the heart of the tumultuous bar, Hoppy proceeded with cautious steps, skillfully threading through the labyrinth of animated conversations and clinking drinkware.

"I see the bar," Hoppy declared with a touch of triumph, his gaze piercing through the colorful throng that engulfed them.

"Good," Greenie's voice, a gentle whisper from beneath the safety of Hoppy's hat, assured him.

As they neared the bar counter, Hoppy couldn't suppress his curiosity any longer. "How will I recognize her?" he inquired, his eyes scanning the bustling surroundings.

Greenie's response was swift, brimming with confidence, "Because there is only one bartender that works here."

Despite the anticipation, when Hoppy cast his gaze upon the bar, his hopeful expectations weren't met. "She's not here," he uttered with a hint of disappointment.

"She'll be back. She rarely leaves this spot," Greenie reassured, his words imbued with the wisdom of one who knew the rhythm of this place.

Taking Greenie's advice to heart, Hoppy claimed a vacant bar stool, swiveling it to face the animated expanse of the room. "What a crowd," he commented, his eyes trailing over the dynamic assembly.

"It wasn't always like this," Greenie's tone carried a trace of melancholy, "Ever since the pirates took control of the central banking, they extended their grip to this place as well."

Eager for more information, Hoppy probed further, "How long have the pirates been here?"

Before Greenie could answer, a voice, laden with a mixture of fatigue and resolve, chimed in from behind Hoppy's back, "It's been seven long years."

Startled, Hoppy swiveled around, his eyes meeting the gaze of none other than the lizard—the very bartender Greenie had mentioned.

"Seven years of pirates and their reign," she continued, a glint of weary determination in her eyes. "But we hold onto hope, knowing that one day, this bar will be free again."

Perched upon a raised platform behind the bar, the lizard greeted Hoppy with a faint, tired smile. "What can I get you?" she inquired, her voice a testament to the trials she'd witnessed.

"It's her," Greenie's voice confirmed, a note of satisfaction present.

Undeterred by the unusual request, Hoppy ordered milk, all the while admiring the intricate tattoos that adorned the lizard's arms. His gaze wandered to the diamond necklace that graced her neck and the delicate triangle earrings that glimmered in the dim light. The lizard's unconventional beauty didn't escape his attention.

"Milk? Who orders milk at a bar?" Greenie couldn't resist a playful comment, his voice laced with amusement at Hoppy's choice.

With the lizard taking the lead, she suggested a more conventional alternative. "How about a coke?"

"That sounds perfect," Hoppy agreed, his gaze never leaving the bartender who seemed to hold a mysterious air about her.

Noticing the oversized jacket draped over Hoppy's form, the lizard couldn't help but inquire, "Where did you find that jacket?"

"In a lost and found box," Hoppy explained.

Greenie, sensing a connection, shared a quiet revelation, "She recognized the jacket."

Once Hoppy's fountain Coke was prepared, the lizard bartender leaned in, ready to engage in conversation. "I sense that you're new here. So, what brings you to our island?" she inquired, genuine curiosity glinting in her eyes.

Quick on the draw, Greenie fed Hoppy a response through their hidden connection. "Tell her about that old book you read as a kid," he suggested. Hoppy took the cue, sharing, "I stumbled upon an ancient book that spoke of this island when I was younger."

Impressed by the tale, the lizard offered the Coke as a gesture of hospitality, a smile playing at the corner of her lips. Grateful, Hoppy accepted the drink, savoring the refreshing cold liquid as he commented, "There's truly nothing like a good cold Coke."

As the conversation flowed, the lizard learned about the cryptic message Hoppy had uncovered. With an intriguing blend of amusement and curiosity, she listened as Hoppy repeated the enigmatic lines, "If a tinker were my trade, would you still find me, carrying the pots I made, following behind me?"

In an instant, recognition dawned upon the bartender's face, transforming her expression from puzzlement to realization. "Where is he?" she inquired urgently.

Seizing the moment with a hint of mischief, Greenie introduced Hoppy to her. "Hoppy, allow me to introduce you to my ex-wife, Lagartha," he said, his eyes carrying a nostalgic gleam.

Secretly, Hoppy signaled to Lagartha, indicating that her vigilant protector, Greenie, remained concealed beneath his hat, shielded from prying eyes. "Keep him hidden. Revealing Greenie would be disastrous—these pirates would tear him apart," Hoppy whispered.

"He actually said that?" Hoppy shared the exchange with Lagartha.

Greenie's response carried a lighthearted smile, "It's as if we share a mind."

"He mentioned that you two think alike," Hoppy relayed, enjoying the playful banter between the two.

"Tell him to be quiet," Lagartha's tone held a touch of command.

"She says—" Hoppy began to repeat.

"Yeah, got it," Greenie interjected, rescuing Hoppy from repeating Lagartha's instruction.

Turning her attention back to Hoppy, Lagartha aimed to learn more about her new ally. "What's your name, kid?" she asked, her gaze scrutinizing his features.

"Hoppy," he responded, a note of pride in his tone.

Lagartha couldn't resist a playful comment, "A Kangaroo, right?"

Hoppy nodded, "Exactly," confirming his species.

Ever the vigilant strategist, Lagartha quickly formulated an escape plan, guiding them toward safety. "There's a back door on your left. Slip out through there. You'll spot a large wooden dumpster. Wait for me there," she instructed, fully aware that the dark alleyways offered a brief respite from the hazards of the bar's interior.

As if a shadow navigating the night, Hoppy moved gracefully toward the back door, ensuring Greenie's secrecy beneath his hat. Once outside, the cacophony of the bar was replaced by the chill of the open air, welcoming them to their temporary refuge.

Spotting the substantial wooden dumpster nearby, Hoppy couldn't help but inject a bit of humor, "Seems like someone forgot to take out the trash."

Greenie, still discreetly tucked under the hat, peeked at the dumpster and explained, "It's not really trash; it's a disguise. By appearing full and emitting an unpleasant odor, it gives the illusion that no one's been here in a while."

"Greenie?" Hoppy's soft voice reached out.

"Yeah?" came the reply.

"I've got, like, a million questions buzzing in my head," Hoppy admitted, his curiosity ignited by the thrilling events of the evening.

Greenie heaved a sigh, "I understand, and I appreciate your thirst for answers. But I want you to know how much I value what you've done. Whatever comes next, your help means the world. Still, things are going to get dangerous, and you've already held up your end of the bargain. If you decide to leave now, I'd understand."

"Thank you, Greenie, but we're in this together. Going back home isn't an option. Meeting you was a game-changer for me. I'm sticking by my buddy. Plus, you've got two more wishes to use," Hoppy declared, the depth of his loyalty shining through and sealing their bond.

"Thanks, Hoppy. I hoped you'd stay. Your unique abilities will be a game-changer against Zunga and his crew," Greenie expressed his genuine gratitude.

Intrigued by the shadowy adversaries they were up against, Hoppy delved, "What exactly are they after?"

"Who?" Greenie sought clarification.

"Zunga and the others," Hoppy clarified, a hunger for knowledge driving his inquiry.

Greenie revealed the ominous truth, "There are three pirate groups, along with Zunga, that together form the infamous Pirate Club. Each group has specific roles based on their skills. Zunga, in particular, is after something incredibly dangerous that I developed in a lab twenty-five years ago."

"Intriguing, but why create something so perilous?" Hoppy probed further, his curiosity unfazed.

Greenie's tone grew somber as he recounted a distant past, "Thirty-five years ago, a deadly virus-infected weed began to spread across the fertile lands of the Midwest—the same lands supplying forty percent of our food. We named it Plant Z. We had no option but to formulate a chemical to combat its rapid growth, saving our crops and people from the threat of famine."

"And then what?" Hoppy encouraged Greenie to share more of the story.

"After pouring the chemical at Plant Z's roots, it died, but it killed everything it touched, turning the land into a barren wasteland. The chemical remained in the soil, causing devastation for years. Eventually, we managed to bring back the agriculture land with the help of modified mushrooms I secretly grew, but the danger still lurked in the shadows. To ensure it wouldn't fall into the wrong hands, we kept a small bottle of our creation hidden in the Central Banking building on this island," Greenie concluded, his words heavy with the weight of the past.

As Hoppy grappled with the magnitude of Greenie's revelation, Lagartha's voice cut through his thoughts like a lifeline. "Apologies for the wait, Hoppy. Follow me," her tone a mixture of command and reassurance. With determination etched onto her face, she took the lead, navigating the intricate labyrinth of treacherous alleys that defined the dangerous bars.

While Hoppy tried to concentrate on the mission at hand, he couldn't help but feel a swell of pride and curiosity when Lagartha offered an unexpected compliment, "A walking kangaroo, and I thought I'd seen it all." The recognition of his unique abilities warmed his heart, solidifying his role as a crucial member of this audacious alliance.

As they turned a corner, Hoppy's attention was drawn to an unassuming wooden dumpster. Yet, a subtle detail caught his eye—

a barely noticeable seam along one side, a mark that only a keen observer would detect. Lagartha's precise actions betrayed the dumpster's true nature. She knocked with a specific rhythm, and to Hoppy's amazement, the ordinary-looking dumpster transformed into a concealed entrance to a bomb shelter.

From within, a small mole emerged, his diminutive paws gripping the edges of the opening. Gray streaks amidst his dark fur hinted at his age, while his whiskers quivered with excitement. His eyes, though small, exuded wisdom and cunning. His chipper voice belied his years as he inquired, "Is he here?"

Greenie, tucked under Hoppy's hat, cautiously lifted it slightly to greet the mole.

"Hello, Mr. Cellars," Greenie whispered.

The mole's eyes widened in surprise. "Ah, Greenie!" Mr. Cellars responded, his voice tinged with relief. "Quick, come on in before anyone spots you."

"I'm afraid I have to return to the bar," Lagartha interjected, urgency in her voice. "But don't fret; I'll catch up with you later." With a swift turn, she vanished into the obscurity of the alley's shadows.

Following Mr. Cellars, Greenie, and Hoppy scurried through a narrow tunnel that seemed to lead them further into the heart of the island. Soon, they found themselves in a hidden underground refuge. The air was cool and damp, carrying the earthy scent of the subterranean world that surrounded them.

The shelter's interior was bathed in a dim, golden glow, cast by the flickering lanterns that adorned the walls. The soft light illuminated the room, revealing piles of books and meticulously arranged maps resting on makeshift shelves. The space managed to strike a balance between order and coziness, creating an atmosphere that was both inviting and functional.

"I apologize for the secrecy, but it's not safe for creatures like us to be seen above ground these days," Mr. Cellars explained, his voice laced with concern and the weight of responsibility.

Greenie nodded in understanding, fully aware of the lurking dangers that existed beyond the shelter's confines. "Thank you for offering us refuge, Mr. Cellars."

Mr. Cellars responded with a warm smile, his eyes reflecting a genuine commitment to his role. "It's my duty to safeguard fellow creatures from harm. Now, let me guide you around and introduce you to some other inhabitants of this sanctuary. They might be able to provide valuable insights for your journey."

Following Mr. Cellars through a labyrinth of interconnected tunnels, their movements were as hushed as the rustling of leaves in a gentle breeze. Their paws and webbed feet brushed silently against the cool, damp earth, leaving almost no trace of their passage.

"You know, Greenie," the mole spoke softly, his voice carrying a sense of nostalgia, "I remember the old you."

Greenie cast a thoughtful gaze at Mr. Cellars, a mix of emotions flickering in his eyes. "Being a frog comes with its challenges," he admitted, his words infused with a subtle yearning.

The mole paused, his eyes lingering on Greenie's amphibian form. "You used to be quite different," he mused, a wistful tone underlying his words. "You were someone else entirely." A sigh escaped him, a blend of sorrow and empathy coloring his expression.

Curiosity burning in his chest, Hoppy interjected, "What does he mean, Greenie? You were someone else?"

Greenie exchanged a quick, meaningful glance with Hoppy, a reassuring smile playing on his lips. "It's a story for another time, Hoppy," he replied, leaving the details for a future conversation.

At last, they stood before a stout wooden door, and with a gentle push of his claw, Mr. Cellars ushered them inside.

The room was adorned with soft lantern light, creating an ambiance of quiet determination. Three moles were gathered around a large table, covered in maps, blueprints, and intricate island sketches. As the door swung open, their attention snapped towards it, their eyes lighting up with anticipation.

"Greenie! You're back!" exclaimed a mole wearing spectacles perched on his snout. His voice was a mixture of relief and excitement, reflecting their shared trust and camaraderie.

A surge of warmth and connection filled Greenie as he responded, "I'm glad to be back, Coast."

The second mole, with a nimble demeanor and a quick wit, chimed in, "Perfect timing!"

The third mole, a figure of wisdom and experience, nodded in agreement.

With a renewed determination gleaming in his eyes, Greenie addressed his allies, his tone infused with urgency. "Frankie, James, it's good to see you both. Time is of the essence. The longer those pirates remain in control, the more damage they wreak upon our beloved island."

Chapter Nine

The Pirates' Lair

The bustling streets of Central Island were a dynamic backdrop as the raccoons scurried with a sense of purpose, bearing Zunga's heavy chest in their nimble paws. Zunga's towering figure led the procession, his very presence casting a shadow of dominance over his obedient subordinates. Clutched firmly in his powerful hand was a birdcage, within which Rocco fluttered with a mix of apprehension and curiosity.

Zunga's muscular arms swung in a rhythm that matched his stride, an embodiment of his commanding strength and imposing aura. Amidst the activity, Rocco's cheerful chirps resonated, as if he reveled in the vibrancy of the island's surroundings. His vibrant feathers glimmered under the sunlight, each flutter causing the cage to sway and Rocco's small frame to bob in response.

The inquisitive nature of the bird got the best of him, prompting him to strike up an unexpected conversation with Zunga. With mischief dancing in his eyes, Rocco drew closer to Zunga and chirped playfully, "So, what's the secret to becoming a pirate these days?"

Zunga, meeting Rocco's gaze with a gaze of his own, allowed a hint of nostalgia to touch his expression. The corners of his lips curled into a knowing smile as he spoke with authority, "To be a pirate, one must harbor an insatiable craving for adventure and an unquenchable thirst for freedom," his voice resonating with a wisdom that spoke of his experiences.

The closer Zunga led them to the Central Building, the more vivid the scene became. The island's colors seemed to burst forth, a symphony of vibrant hues that painted the backdrop to their journey. The air carried the enticing scent of exotic spices, and in the distance, the rhythmic crash of waves against the shore contributed to the enchantment of the moment.

As the Central Building loomed ahead, its grandeur was marred by the pirates' occupation, transforming it into their secretive stronghold. The structure, now bedecked with weathered pirate flags, stood as a testament to their supremacy. Yet, despite the pirate's conquest, the building's outer facade retained an air of elegance and allure, capturing the attention of all who passed by.

The architectural marvel of the Central Building was an undeniable spectacle. Its facade bore intricate designs and ornate carvings that immediately seized Rocco's attention. The sheer scale of the structure, coupled with its majestic splendor, created an irresistible presence that drew gazes and admiration.

Zunga's voice reverberated, commanding Rocco's attention as he issued a clear directive, ensuring that his message was understood. "Listen up, little bird. If you know what's good for you, you'll keep your beak shut and behave. No funny business, got it?"

"I promise, Zunga. My beak will stay sealed. Just let me warble my tunes, and I'll keep the peace," Rocco responded, his voice tinged with a mix of innocence and compliance.

Zunga's menacing gaze bore down on Rocco, his piercing eyes locking onto the canary for a moment before a low grunt of approval rumbled from his throat. "Good. You can sing your heart out, but not a single word. Remember, one false note, and you'll find yourself in the belly of my Chango. Understood? Cross me, and you'll pay the price."

Rocco's tiny heart raced within his chest as he nodded in response. The weight of his survival rested heavily on his feathered shoulders, and he was acutely aware of the consequences of any misstep.

Stepping through a nondescript side entrance, the interior of the lair was unveiled before Rocco's watchful eyes. A bustling scene greeted him, a chaotic ballet of pirates of varying statures and builds, each with their own purpose. Some transported pilfered riches in tattered sacks, while others huddled in conspiratorial groups, plotting their next wicked escapade. The once bustling bank employees were now hostages to the pirate horde, their movements marked by apprehension and resignation.

The room pulsed with frenetic energy, pirates bustling in and out through different passages. The mingling aromas of salt-laden air and potent rum wafted through the chamber, intertwining with the mustiness of aging parchments and gleaming gold. The flickering candlelight cast eerie and elongated shadows that danced upon the timeworn wallpaper, creating a surreal and almost mystical atmosphere.

Guided by Zunga's imposing presence, his raccoon companions deftly navigated the chaos, eliciting both reverence and dread from those who crossed their path. Pirates, recognizing their leader, hastily stepped aside, granting a wide berth for their passage. The bank employees, caught in a struggle between duty and terror, cast wary glances, a blend of curiosity and fear accompanying their gaze.

Amid the tumultuous scene, Rocco's melodious chirps reverberated through the air, a burst of vibrant color amidst the dimly lit surroundings. The canary's cage swayed gently in Zunga's grip, the delicate movement a stark juxtaposition to the pirate's imposing presence.

Upon reaching the heart of the lair, Zunga positioned himself at the center of the room, his authoritative figure demanding the attention of all present. "Pirates!" His commanding voice reverberated through the space, the rumbling tone asserting his dominance.

The room fell into an anticipatory silence, every eye turned toward their formidable leader, eager to hear his next decree. The atmosphere was charged with a blend of intrigue and tension, the rugged countenances of the pirates and the anxiety etched onto the employees' faces creating a palpable sense of anticipation.

"Pirates!" Zunga's voice resonated again, a potent declaration that commanded respect. "Gather close, for I bear tidings of utmost significance."

Zunga's voice, both commanding and sly, cut through the atmosphere like a dagger. "Zatarh, the ancient witch rat, is my captive," he announced with an ominous grin that twisted his features. "She languishes in my dungeon, where her misdeeds shall bear their weight."

A ripple of mingled fear and triumph coursed through the assembled crowd. Zatarh, a legendary figure known for her sorcery and cunning, held sway over the collective imagination. To have captured her was a significant accomplishment, a feat that cemented Zunga's reputation as a force to be reckoned with.

"But heed my warning," Zunga's voice deepened, dripping with a chilling foreboding. "Two of Zatarh's cunning sisters remain at large. Dangerous and shrouded in darkness, we must remain watchful."

Glances exchanged among the pirates were laden with shared unease, the weight of the task ahead apparent. The pursuit of the remaining witches necessitated not only courage but strategic prowess.

"And now," Zunga's tone took on a tantalizing edge, "one of the four coveted yellow diamonds has fallen into our grasp."

Avarice ignited within the eyes of the pirates, the gleam of unbridled desire igniting their spirits. The legendary yellow diamonds were prized beyond measure, coveted by fortune seekers from across the globe.

"Prepare yourselves," Zunga's command sliced through the charged atmosphere. "Secure the witch rats, seize the remaining diamonds – these are our priorities."

Rocco, imprisoned within his cage, felt a pang of concern grip his heart. His voice stifled, he absorbed the weight of his captivity, yet it was Zunga's ominous words that truly troubled him. Their echo reverberated in his mind, a harbinger of impending danger and uncertainty.

With Zunga's pronouncement concluded, the building burst back to life. Pirates resumed their tasks, and employees scurried about, each driven by the gravity of their leader's directives. Rocco's cage was placed on the front desk counter, a temporary haven in the midst of bustling activity, yet still a symbol of captivity.

Turning his attention to a fox employee, Zunga's command cut through the frenetic energy. "Frank, keep a vigilant eye on this chatty bird," he instructed, gesturing to Rocco's enclosure. "No shenanigans while I'm away."

Frank, a mixture of apprehension and resolve etched onto his features, nodded dutifully. "You can count on me," he replied, his voice a mix of deference and determination. "I'll ensure he remains well-behaved."

Within the cage, Rocco's feathers ruffled with a mixture of frustration and resolve. Lifting his gaze to meet Zunga's eyes, he summoned his bravery and managed to utter a plea, "May I speak again, Zunga? I assure you, I'll be on my best behavior."

Zunga's eyes bore into the tiny canary confined within the cage, his calculating stare giving way to a begrudging nod of agreement. His command was swift and unwavering. "Maroony, Looney, follow me," he ordered, his voice holding a blend of authority and expectation. With a mixture of fear and obedience, the two raccoons scurried after their leader, their nimble paws straining under the weight of the chest they carried.

Meanwhile, Rocco, his cage resting on the front desk counter, turned his attention to Frank, the fox employee stationed nearby. "Frank, right?" Rocco chirped, his voice a mixture of curiosity and recognition.

In the hidden recesses of the island, a secret sanctuary was the gathering place for four moles, Mr. Cellars, Frankie, and James, along with their steadfast companion Greenie. The underground chamber was softly illuminated by flickering lanterns, the warm glow casting a sense of camaraderie and purpose among the group. Within the cozy enclave, discussions buzzed with the energy of anticipation, a palpable excitement infusing the air.

Around a robust wooden table, the moles and Greenie huddled closely, their eyes intently focused on a set of meticulously detailed blueprints. The play of light and shadow danced upon their resolute faces, a testament to their determination as they strategized, each sip of tea a comforting reassurance in the face of the challenging task that lay ahead.

Studying the intricate blueprints, Coast, his spectacles perched on his snout, turned his inquisitive gaze toward Greenie. A paw gestured toward Hoppy, inviting an introduction. "Greenie, who might this young friend of yours be?"

Greenie's expression held a mixture of pride and fondness as he motioned for Hoppy to step forward. "Allow me to introduce you to Hoppy, the walking Kangaroo," he announced with a touch of admiration. "Hoppy possesses remarkable agility and strength, qualities that make him a formidable addition to our mission."

Hoppy, standing tall and resolute, met the curious stares of the moles with a warm and friendly smile. "Greetings, dear friends," he greeted them, his voice imbued with sincerity and camaraderie.

The moles exchanged knowing glances, a realization dawning upon them that this was the missing piece they had been seeking. Their attention focused on Hoppy, and Mr. Cellars squinted slightly, his gaze assessing. "Tell us, young Hoppy, how many years have you lived?"

Caught slightly off guard by the question, Hoppy responded, "I am 14 years old."

A look of intrigue crossed Mr. Cellars' features, his gaze sharpening. Leaning in, he inquired further, "Were you brought into this world on the fifth day of January?"

Surprise flickered across Hoppy's features. How could Mr. Cellars possibly know his exact birthdate? Uncertainty tugged at his thoughts, but he decided to answer truthfully. "Yes, that's correct

With a enigmatic smile, Mr. Cellars responded, "Ah, my dear friends, there is much more to this tale than meets the eye." A brief pause followed, his gaze a mix of sagacity and playfulness. "You see, my companions, the alignment of stars and the positions of celestial bodies can unveil connections beyond our comprehension." He paused, letting the weight of his words settle in. "Hoppy's birthdate holds a hidden rapport with a potent force that slumbers within him."

Hoppy and Greenie exchanged baffled glances, their minds grappling to grasp the profoundness of Mr. Cellars' revelation.

Sensing their bewilderment, Mr. Cellars carried on, his voice a soothing guide through the enigma. "Hoppy, our Kangaroo friend, you are graced with a singular talent, a boon bequeathed by the cosmos. Your birth coincides with a rare cosmic phenomenon, bestowing upon you the remarkable ability to walk upright."

Hoppy's eyes widened with wonder. This newfound insight breathed purpose into his being, offering him an understanding of why he stood distinct from his Kangaroo peers.

However, it was Greenie, his expression knotted with intrigue, who posed the question that danced at the edges of their understanding. "Mr. Cellars, does this relate to the incident fourteen years ago, when the world's axes shifted for a mere 30 seconds?"

Mr. Cellars turned toward Greenie, a knowing gleam in his eyes. "Indeed, my steadfast friend. That event left a considerable imprint on our world. The abrupt shift caused the moon's tides to alter, yet that was merely the beginning. An even more extraordinary occurrence unfolded for a select few born precisely fourteen years ago on January 5th, during those fleeting moments."

Greenie's curiosity bloomed into full-fledged intrigue. "What happened to them, Mr. Cellars? Was it a kind of enchantment?"

With a nod, Mr. Cellars continued, his voice imbued with a sense of wonder. "Certainly. Their DNA underwent an enigmatic transformation, redefining their very essence. They seemed to be touched by the cosmic forces unleashed during those brief moments of celestial tumult."

The logical next question hung in the air, poised upon Greenie's lips. "But what implications does this hold for those who were affected?"

Mr. Cellars let out a knowing chuckle, his paw stroking his whiskers in contemplation. "That, my friends, remains the enigma. The nature of these alterations is yet to be unraveled."

As the profundity of this information settled within them, Hoppy's thoughts swirled with a whirlwind of inquiries. An undercurrent of exhilaration merged with a hint of trepidation. What hidden facets of his being had yet to be uncovered? And how would this extraordinary endowment shape the path he was destined to tread?

Chapter Ten

Roundtable

In the heart of the hidden island, where the sun's golden fingers stretched out in a farewell embrace, Mr. Cellars perceived the rhythmic cadence of knocks upon the shelter's door. The dim chamber hummed with anticipation, shadows flickering like old tales coming to life. With a knowing glance, he turned to his companions, Hoppy and Greenie. His whiskers trembled with excitement. "It must be Lagartha," he whispered, a conspiratorial twinkle in his eye. Hoppy and Greenie exchanged eager looks, mirroring the shared curiosity that pulsed within them. Together, they followed Mr. Cellars to the entrance, where the door creaked open like the gateway to destiny.

And there she stood, resplendent in her shimmering emerald scales—a living testament to the island's secrets. Lagartha's eyes, a mosaic of urgency and resolve, bore a message that dared not wait. "The others have gathered and are waiting," she announced, her voice carrying the weight of necessity. "We must embark immediately."

Mr. Cellars nodded, his gaze a reflection of his unwavering determination. "Go on ahead," he instructed, his voice a steady anchor. "I shall join you in due time."

As if guided by an invisible hand, Greenie sprang from his perch, landing lithely on Hoppy's shoulder. His sly maneuver to secure his place beneath the hat, however, was thwarted by fate's whims. Lagartha's gaze collided with his, a moment of unexpected recognition and history between them. Yet, Greenie, never one to waste an opportunity, swiftly pivoted with a glint of mischief and extended his hand in invitation. "Would you care to accompany me?" he inquired, a wistful note softening his words.

Lagartha paused, caught between the currents of memories and present circumstances. The warm, orange hues of the waning sun painted her emerald scales in ethereal light. For all the differences that had once torn them apart, there remained the echo of shared adventures and unspoken understanding. With a tender smile, she nodded, a nod to the past as much as the present. "Why not?" she agreed, the word a bridge between past and present.

But as their connection rekindled, a sudden eruption of sound shattered the fragile moment, cutting through the air like a clarion call. They turned, gazes lifting to the heavens, where a majestic silhouette danced against the canvas of sky—a figure both ominous and magnificent. Chango, Zunga's cunning crow, glided with the grace of shadows, a harbinger of urgency. A tinge of foreboding gripped Lagartha as the significance of this unexpected visitor etched itself into her consciousness. "We must hasten," she urged, her voice trembling with a mix of determination and anxiety. "There's no time to waste."

In the heart of the bustling island, nestled within the grand walls of the central bank building, Zunga found himself seated in a lavishly furnished office. An air of tension enveloped him as he anxiously awaited the arrival of the three other pirate leaders, all summoned to gather around the imposing round table. The opulent room was adorned with maps of uncharted territories, mysterious artifacts, and shelves lined with rare books. Sunlight streamed through the stained-glass windows, casting vibrant patterns that danced across the walls.

Amidst the opulence of the lavishly furnished office, the polished roundtable cradled the chest housing one of the fabled yellow diamonds. Zunga's gaze remained unwavering, his focus tethered to the precious gem resting before him. His faithful raccoon attendants, vigilant in their loyalty, remained at his side, their presence an extension of his own commanding aura. A subtle gesture of his fingers released them from his side, dispatching them to stand guard outside the door.

Then, as if a tempest brewed in the corridor beyond, a sudden tumult unfurled. The noise of shuffling footsteps crescendoed, echoing through the thick door and reverberating within the room. Zunga's raccoon companions, attuned to the discord, hastened to evacuate the scene, leaving him alone with the impending unknown. With the charged silence of a seasoned pirate captain, his steely gaze pierced through the closed door.

The heavy wooden door creaked open, and the atmosphere in the room shifted as the first of the pirate leaders made his entrance. Captain Brive, a hyena with a lean and powerful physique, stood tall, exuding an air of undeniable confidence. His eyes twinkled mischievously, and a bandana wrapped snugly around his head added to his enigmatic charm. The faint scent of saltwater clung to his attire, a reminder of the ever-present sea that shaped his adventurous spirit. With each step he took, he commanded attention, capturing the gaze of everyone present.

"Zunga, my friend, I see you're as punctual as ever," Captain Brive remarked, a smirk dancing on his lips as he glanced at the chest resting on the table before him.

Zunga, equally cunning and charismatic, responded with a sly grin of his own. "You know me too well, Brive. Time waits for no pirate, especially when great stakes are on the line." His voice held a husky edge.

The door swung open once more, and a vibrant, fierce figure burst into the room. It was none other than Captain Scarlet, a red fox with an electrifying presence. Her fiery red locks cascaded down her shoulders like a blazing waterfall, accentuating her agile and powerful physique. The soft rustling of her crimson coat seemed to echo the untamed spirit that radiated from her. Every step she took oozed self-assurance, captivating the attention of everyone in the room. Her emerald eyes sparkled with mischief, revealing a cunning and adventurous spirit that sent shivers down the spines of all who beheld her.

"Apologies for my tardiness," she chimed in, her voice dripping with sarcasm. The playful glint in her eyes mirrored her witty tone. "I had to make sure our ship was ready for anything that might come our way."

Zunga waved off her apology, his eyes never leaving the chest on the table. "No worries, Scarlet. We have much to discuss." The anticipation in his voice was palpable, mirroring the unspoken thrill that hung in the air.

Before any further words could be exchanged, the doors swung open again, revealing the final pirate leader, Captain Steelheart, an immense tiger with a commanding presence. His cold gaze and a gleaming metal arm in the dim light only added to the aura of power and mystery surrounding him. The room seemed to shrink in his presence as his sheer presence dominated the space. The weathered scars on his face bore witness to countless battles, a testament to his relentless and fierce nature. The tiger's striped fur seemed to ripple like flames in the shadows, making him appear both majestic and dangerous.

As he locked eyes with Zunga, a silent acknowledgment of their shared history passed between them, and he took his seat at the table, his movements fluid and deliberate. "Zunga," Steelheart spoke in a calm yet authoritative tone, his deep voice resonating through the room. "I presume this meeting holds great significance, considering you've summoned us all here."

Zunga's grin widened, his eyes gleaming with excitement like a child who's discovered a hidden treasure. "Indeed, Steelheart. We stand on the verge of our greatest conquest yet, and this chest holds the key to our success." The eagerness in his voice matched the spark that danced in his eyes, both fueled by the grandiosity of their ambitions.

"You all must have heard by now," Zunga's voice was low and gravelly, his words carrying an air of secrecy and excitement, "I was able to secure one of the four legendary yellow diamonds we've been relentlessly searching for."

The pirates exchanged intrigued glances, their eyes gleaming with a mix of greed and anticipation. Captain Brive leaned forward, his eyes shining with the thrill of the chase. "One diamond in our hands, mates," he declared, his voice gruff but commanding. "But we won't rest until we secure the other two and complete our operation."

Zunga's grin widened, his eyes flickering with a fire of determination. "Yes, we only need two more diamonds to start our mission. The other three diamonds remain hidden, waiting for us to claim them. But first, we must uncover their secret locations."

Captain Steelheart, an enigmatic figure with a mysterious past hidden behind his scars, nodded in agreement, his cold gaze reflecting a sense of understanding. "Aye, Captain, but where do we start?"

Zunga tapped his fingers thoughtfully on the table, the sound echoing in the room as he considered the question. "We've heard of a hidden island, deep within the treacherous Blue Lagoon," he finally revealed. "Legend has it that this island holds the whereabouts of one of the diamonds. The journey won't be easy, but the rewards are worth the risk."

Scarlet, her fiery red hair cascading over her face like a waterfall of flames, spoke up with a fierce determination that matched her appearance. "You're talking about the island of the forgotten, aren't you?"

Zunga nodded to Scarlet, acknowledging her astute guess.

Captain Brive interjected, a hint of concern in his voice, "But what about the dangers that await us on the island? How will we navigate through them?"

Zunga's smile held a touch of mystery, his confidence unwavering. "Fear not. We have an invaluable prisoner who knows the secrets of that island. Zatara, the elusive witch rat, is now our captive in the depths of my ship's dungeon. She will be our guide, ensuring our safe passage through the perils that lie ahead."

Steelheart leaned forward, his intense gaze fixed on Zunga. "Can we trust her?" he questioned with a mixture of skepticism and caution.

The pirates leaned in, their curiosity piqued by the mention of the enigmatic witch rat. Zunga continued, his voice resolute, "Zatara has confessed that she has concealed one diamond deep within the mystical blue lagoon. It was not easy to make her talk, but everyone breaks when they have a soft spot, and the witch broke," Zunga added with an unsettling smile, revealing a side of him that was both cunning and ruthless.

Captain Brive inquired, his curiosity mirrored in his furrowed brow, "What about Zatara's sisters?"

Zunga's determination remained unshaken, his eyes burning with a relentless resolve. "While they deceived us about the sisters' hiding locations, we won't be deterred. Each sister holds knowledge of a specific yellow diamond's location, and we must find them at any cost. Your brother, Trigger, is assigned that mission. I am confident he will not fail to locate them the next time."

Captain Steelheart leaned forward, his intense gaze fixed on Zunga. "Zunga," he spoke in a low, gravelly voice that carried a weight of seriousness, "have you managed to secure the synthetic seeds from Dr. Lintage?"

Zunga met Captain Steelheart's eyes head-on, exuding confidence. "Yes, Captain," he replied with authority, his deep voice resonating across the table. "I journeyed to Blanta, the bustling city of Bjmen, where the brilliant scientist Squirrel had been working. He had two dozen barrels of those precious synthetic seeds awaiting me. We made sure he was safely reunited with his family."

Suddenly, a tap resonated from the window, a sharp sound that cut through the conversation and startled everyone in the room. Zunga's loyal crow, Chango, had arrived. Zunga promptly excused himself and stood up, his massive frame casting a commanding presence over the space. With practiced ease, he made his way to the window, pushing it open to allow Chango's entry. The crow gracefully landed on Zunga's broad shoulder, leaning in to whisper urgently in the pirate's ear. "An observant individual caught sight of the frog," Chango conveyed with a sense of urgency.

Zunga's eyes narrowed, fully focused on Chango's message. The gravity of the news sank in as he absorbed every word, his mind already racing with thoughts of the challenges and opportunities that lay ahead.

In the center of the bustling Central Building, an eclectic mix of pirates, mobs, employees, and other curious characters had gathered around, forming a diverse and entertained audience.

Laughter rang out, filling the air as Rocco, the vibrant canary, held court from his perch on the counter. His captivated audience hung on his every word as he animatedly recounted his daring escapades.

"So there I was," Rocco began, his voice infused with a contagious enthusiasm that swept through the crowd. "I took him on a wild goose chase, zigzagging from right to left faster than a squirrel on roller skates. And just when he thought he had me cornered, I executed a maneuver so swift that he didn't even have time to blink! I punched him right, then I punched him left, and before he even knew what hit him, I grabbed him by his throat and stuck him into the ground!"

Gasps of amazement swept through the crowd, eyes wide with disbelief as they hung onto every word. Rocco paused, letting the suspense build before continuing, a playful spark dancing in his eyes. "And you know what the snake said to me?" he asked, lowering his voice to a conspiratorial whisper. "He looked at me and said, 'I have never seen a kung fu master move so fast!'"

The eruption of laughter was infectious, spreading like wildfire among the listeners. Even the tough pirates and hardened mobsters couldn't help but chuckle at Rocco's audacious tale. The curious crowd hungered for more, one voice breaking through the mirth, "What kind of snake was it?" the voice asked, curiosity lacing every word.

Rocco, undaunted by the challenge, beamed with confidence as he responded, "Oh, it was a Cobra, my friends. But not just any Cobra, mind you, a sleek and mysterious golden one!"

The laughter grew even louder, the amusement reaching new heights as Rocco's storytelling prowess shone. However, the boisterous atmosphere took an abrupt turn as Zunga, the imposing pirate leader, gracefully maneuvered through the crowd. All eyes turned to him as he fixated on the birdcage that held Rocco captive, the storyteller's performance coming to an unexpected halt. The sudden silence was palpable as Zunga's stern expression cast a serious air over the previously festive scene.

With a decisive tone, Zunga declared, "The show is over." The atmosphere shifted instantly, and the bustling activity of the Central Building resumed as if nothing unusual had happened. The incongruity between the joyful laughter moments ago and the sudden return to business as usual was stark.

Yet, despite the return to normalcy, the glint of mischief in Zunga's eyes was unmistakable as he peered at Rocco through the confines of the cage. His authoritative voice carried a sense of urgency as he posed a question that cut through the air like a blade, "Where might the frog and his Kangaroo friend be?"

Rocco's heart pounded as the weight of the question settled upon him. He swallowed hard, his feathers ruffled with anxiety. He knew the stakes were high, and he needed to tread carefully to protect his friends. The pressure was on, and Rocco's mind raced as he searched for a clever response that would keep them safe from the ever-watchful Zunga.

In another part of the island, hidden from prying eyes, Lagartha and Greenie carefully sought refuge under Hoppy's Hat. The clever disguise concealed them as they navigated their way toward a small, unassuming cottage on the outskirts of the bustling city. Each step was deliberate, taken with caution to avoid drawing attention to themselves.

As they approached the cottage, their eyes darted around, vigilant for any signs of potential danger. The surroundings appeared tranquil, devoid of any watchful gazes or suspicious figures. A fleeting sense of security enveloped Lagartha, and she leaned in close to Hoppy, her voice barely audible above the rustling leaves.

"Remember, Hoppy," Lagartha instructed in a hushed tone, her breath creating a mist in the air, "knock three times, then pause. Repeat that sequence three times before concluding with a single, deliberate knock."

Hoppy's anticipation grew as he absorbed Lagartha's guidance. Positioned before the cottage door, he steadied himself, his heart racing with a mix of anxiety and excitement. Lagartha's instructions echoed in his mind as he prepared to execute the covert code. Three knocks, a pause, the pattern repeated twice more, and finally, a single, authoritative knock.

With a soft creak, the door opened, revealing the inviting interior bathed in the warm glow of flickering candlelight. A kind face emerged from within the cottage, belonging to Phillip, a wise old owl. Hoppy exchanged a meaningful look with Lagartha and Greenie, the unspoken confirmation passing between them that they had indeed arrived at the right destination.

"Welcome, Hoppy," Phillip's voice carried a sense of genuine warmth as he greeted the kangaroo. "I've been awaiting your arrival. Please, step inside."

Chapter Eleven

The kangaroo is on the roof

As Hoppy settled into the cozy cottage, he carefully removed his hat, revealing the faces of both Greenie and Lagartha. "Hello, Phillip," Greenie chimed in, his voice carrying genuine warmth, "It's good to see you again." Phillip's eyes lit up with a familiar twinkle as he replied, "Ah, my old friend Greenie, it's always a pleasure to have you here."

Phillip's attention shifted to Greenie's unique amphibian form, his curiosity evident. "It must be quite an adjustment, my dear, being a frog and all."

Greenie let out a thoughtful sigh, nodding in agreement. "You're right, Phillip. Being a frog has its challenges, but I'm learning to embrace it."

With a nod of understanding, Greenie and Lagartha gracefully hopped off of Hoppy's head, joining Phillip as he led them deeper into the welcoming interior of the cottage. "Follow me," Phillip beckoned, his steps sure and confident, "our old friends are waiting for you both. And, of course, we have some delicious food prepared for you. I'm sure you could both use a hearty meal after your journey."

"You've always been a gracious host, Phillip," Greenie responded with gratitude, his appreciation evident in his tone.

As they ventured through a charming hallway adorned with whimsical paintings, Phillip reached a door that opened into the attic space above. Ascending the stairs, a sense of anticipation lingered in the air, mingling with the warmth of friendship and camaraderie. Inside the attic, a lively gathering was in full swing. Lamel, the wise and charismatic monkey, stood proudly with a cane, exuding an air of sage authority. Next to him, a majestic wolf named Dr. Silvershade, his coat shimmering like moonlight, wore an attire that hinted at his intellect and healing expertise. Nearby, a relaxed koala radiated carefree charm, and at the heart of the assembly stood a massive tiger, emanating an undeniable aura of strength and leadership.

The group was deeply engrossed in a conversation of great import, their voices carrying the weight of their shared experiences and purpose. The attic was adorned with an array of peculiar artifacts and relics, each holding a story of thrilling adventures and daring escapades.

As Hoppy and Greenie crossed the threshold, all heads turned to greet them, the energy in the room shifting to one of warmth and camaraderie. Lamel's eyes sparkled with familiarity, and he greeted Greenie with genuine joy, "Greenie, it's so good to see you again!"

Greenie's smile lit up his face even more, "It's good to see you too, Lamel. Your wisdom is always a guiding light."

Dr. Silvershade, the wolf renowned for his intellect and compassion, offered a warm smile. "Ah, Greenie, you bring your unique spirit back to us. It's a pleasure to have you with us again."

Greenie nodded, his respect evident in his gaze. "The pleasure is always mine, Dr. Silvershade. Your wisdom and kindness inspire us all."

The koala, known as Lexar, chimed in with an undeniable enthusiasm, his voice tinged with genuine emotion, "I can't believe you're back, Greenie! We thought we'd lost you forever!"

Greenie's eyes held a glint of deep gratitude as he responded, his voice carrying a hint of relief and wonder, "I thought so too, Lexar, but somehow fate had other plans for me."

Greenie turned his attention to the towering figure of Trigger, a massive tiger whose presence commanded respect and attention. "Trigger," Greenie spoke, his words carrying a blend of admiration and camaraderie, "it's good to see you again."

Trigger's response came with a nod of acknowledgement, his deep voice resonating with a mixture of respect and connection. "Greenie," he replied with a simple yet impactful nod.

With a sense of anticipation and the warm glow of friendship, Greenie's gaze turned to Hoppy, who stood by his side. With a proud smile, he introduced his newfound companion to the assembled group. "Everyone, I'd like you to meet Hoppy, a walking kangaroo. We've navigated through a series of incredible adventures together."

The group turned their attention to Hoppy, his infectious enthusiasm lifting their spirits despite the gravity of their situation. Trigger, embodying wisdom and authority, stepped forward to provide an answer. "Zunga needs Zatarh to locate another diamond," he began. "My brother, Steelheart, is one of Zunga's allies, and he's fixated on the legends of black gold hidden deep within our planet's core. They believe that with three yellow diamonds, they can access this precious treasure, but there are only four known to exist."

Greenie, his admiration for Hoppy growing by the minute, chimed in, "This afternoon, I caught a glimpse of Zunga leaving his ship at the dock. My heart has been set on rescuing Zatarh since I first heard of her abduction, but I couldn't jeopardize my undercover mission."

Hoppy's posed another question, "Did Zunga have a canary with him?"

"Indeed, he did. A feisty little bird named Rocco," he confirmed, "He was locked up in a birdcage."

Upon hearing this, Hoppy's heart swelled with determination. "I must save him," he declared, his eyes shining with bravery and compassion. The young kangaroo was ready to leap into action, driven by the fierce loyalty he felt towards his newfound friend.

Lamel, the venerable and experienced monkey, stepped into the forefront, his aged hand resting reassuringly on Hoppy's robust shoulder. "Undertaking a challenge against Zunga requires meticulous planning," he advised, his voice a steady beacon of both caution and empathy. "He's not to be underestimated – a crafty and perilous adversary. Our approach must be one of caution and precision."

Lexar, the sharp-witted member of the group, interjected with fervor, his eyes agleam with a spark of intellect. "Our strategy must be well-considered and cunning," he offered eagerly. "By observing Zunga's patterns, identifying his vulnerabilities, and then outmaneuvering him, we stand a better chance at success. Trigger, is there a way you can gather intelligence about Rocco's whereabouts?"

Trigger, his resolve unwavering, nodded firmly. "I will ascertain the location where he is held captive," he pledged.

Amidst their discussions, Mr. Philip, with a hint of concern etched in his features, approached Greenie. His eyes held a gentle sincerity as he addressed the matter at hand. "The pirates have set their sights on the formula you crafted twenty-five years ago," he stated softly. "Do you retain knowledge of its hiding place within the central bank building?"

Greenie's expression conveyed a mix of nostalgia and determination. His words held a note of vulnerability as he confessed, "I did not conceal it myself. Lagartha holds that secret; she alone knows the location of the hidden lab tube."

All eyes turned to Lagartha, the intelligent and resourceful lizard, who met their gaze with unwavering assurance. Her response was laced with both confidence and a dash of playfulness. "It looks like Greenie and I have a mission to retrieve the tube," she proclaimed with a glint in her eye. "Piece of cake."

Lexar's agile mind immediately sprung into action, his tone reflective of his quick thinking. "We must formulate a concrete plan. The central bank building poses its challenges, even with Lagartha's exceptional skills. Our approach must be adaptable to any circumstance."

Lamel, seasoned with wisdom and experience, offered his thoughts, "Absolutely. Stealth and strategy are our allies. I'll be ready to seek assistance if the situation takes a perilous turn."

Trigger's formidable presence commanded attention as he spoke with a resonant authority. "Zunga and my deceitful brother, Stealheart, are preparing to embark on their quest for another diamond. But before their nefarious plans unfold, freeing Zatara is paramount. I will gather crucial intelligence on their actions and learn Rocco's location."

Greenie's resolve glimmered anew, a testament to his undeterred commitment. "Together, as a united team, we can prevail," he affirmed, casting a gaze of trust and gratitude toward each member. "Past challenges have proven our resilience."

Turning to Dr. Silvershade, Greenie's tone was one of hope and inquiry. "How advanced is your progress in formulating a counteragent?" he asked, his anticipation palpable.

Dr. Silvershade's eyes gleamed with determination as he responded, "I've got a promising lead. There's potential, but I need to return to the lab and delve deeper into the research. I'll keep you updated on my progress."

"Lagartha, Hoppy, and I have decided to take on the task of scouting the area around the central building. Our goal is to explore the surroundings and uncover any potential entry points that might be lurking. The moles managed to unearth a valuable nugget of information. It turns out that hidden within the depths of old blueprints lies a secret entrance to the building, a discovery that could prove to be our key to entry."

Hoppy interposes, his fervor evident, "And remember, we're not just after the formula; we're also after rescuing Rocco."

With plans set and determination filling the air, Lexar's voice cut through the discussions. "At midnight, we'll convene at the moles' underground shelter," he declared with resolve. "There, we'll merge our insights, constructing the foundation of a formidable strategy to confront Zunga and his crew head-on."

"All right then, it's settled. We'll rendezvous there," Greenie affirmed. Turning to Lagartha and Hoppy, a determined glint in his eye, he continued, "But for now, let's pay a little visit to the central bank."

As the conversation concluded, Philip, the epitome of graciousness, took a step forward. "I'll accompany you to the door," he volunteered, his smile radiating warmth and camaraderie.

Beyond the cottage, the trio embarked on their covert journey towards the central building. Each step was deliberate, their determination resonating in every movement. Greenie and Lagartha remained concealed beneath Hoppy's hat, ready for action. However, within the bounds of their secret mission, Hoppy's curiosity bubbled to the surface. He couldn't resist any longer. "Hey, Greenie," he started, excitement tinging his voice, "I've heard some talk about how you're difficult to spot in this form. What's the story behind that?" Hoppy's inquiry hung in the air, curiosity evident in his tone.

Greenie's gaze shifted to Lagartha, a playful twinkle in his eyes. "Lagartha, why don't you regale our inquisitive kangaroo with the tale?" he proposed with a wink, his excitement evident.

Lagartha nodded, embracing her role as the storyteller. "Hoppy, my friend," she began, her voice carrying the weight of lived experiences, "around eight years ago, there lived a scientist, a panther known for his unwavering dedication to his work and his students. He poured his heart and soul into his research, a passion that unfortunately took a toll on his marriage. Despite the strains, he and his partner managed to maintain a close friendship."

Leaning in, Lagartha's reptilian eyes danced with vivid memories. "On a significant afternoon, the scientist was engrossed in his laboratory, delving into the intricate dance of DNA. His experiments were intricate, involving the fusion of genetic codes from a variety of organisms, with an emphasis on plants. But then, an audacious idea seized him—a leap into the realm of amphibian and reptile DNA."

Her gaze turned introspective, as if she were reliving the past. "He blended DNA from a frog and a lizard, intertwining them like a harmonious symphony. Hoppy, the results were nothing short of miraculous. It was as though the secrets of nature were unveiled right before his eyes."

As Lagartha delved further into the narrative, her tone took on a solemn note. "However, tragedy has a way of slipping in during the most unexpected moments. One sunny afternoon, just as he and his ex-wife were preparing to leave the lab, their world was shattered. The entrance burst open, revealing a band of pirates led by the formidable Zunga."

A shadow passed over Lagartha's features, a mix of regret and anger coloring her words. "In the blink of an eye, their lives spiraled into chaos. Zunga's crew caught them off-guard, and mayhem ensued. The scientist fought valiantly, but Zunga's might was overwhelming. Stealheart, Trigger's brother, held the scientist's ex-wife hostage with a dagger pressed to her throat—a cruel and heart-wrenching twist of fate."

Hoppy leaned in, his eyes wide with rapt attention as the tale unfolded. "And then?" he prompted, his voice a blend of anticipation and concern.

Lagartha's narration continued, painting a vivid tapestry of the unfolding turmoil. "With a chilling grin, Zunga shifted his gaze to the scientist, his eyes gleaming with malevolence. 'Tell me, scientist, where have you hidden the anti-Z formula within the central building?' But the scientist, steadfast and unyielding, met Zunga's gaze with an unwavering silence, a defiant glint shining in his eyes."

As Lagartha's voice grew darker, the tale took a more sinister turn. "Enter Scarlet, a cunning and malevolent fox among the pirates. With deliberate steps, she advanced toward the DNA concoction, a mix of curiosity and avarice dancing in her eyes. Her gaze fixated on a nearby syringe, and without a second thought, she extracted the liquid, beginning with the lizard DNA."

Lagartha's description expertly captured the tension of the moment, keeping her audience on the edge of their seats. "Scarlet's intentions were crystal clear; she was on a mission. Turning her attention back to the scientist, she taunted, 'If words won't loosen your tongue, let's witness how this enigmatic brew affects your cherished wife.' And then, in a heartbeat, the unthinkable occurred – the needle punctured the scientist's ex-wife's skin."

The scene unfolded in a whirlwind of desperation and horror. The scientist's anguished cries reverberated through the air, but his defiance couldn't alter the heart-wrenching reality playing out before him. His ex-wife, frail and lifeless, collapsed to the ground like a discarded marionette, her fate hanging in the balance. The scientist's shouts of despair were a futile plea that seemed to go unheard.

She lay there, seemingly devoid of life, a cruel victim of the pirates' sinister game. The scientist's disbelief was palpable, his heart shattered by the sight that unfolded. Fueled by a surge of adrenaline and rage, he fought against the gang's unyielding grip, every effort met with overpowering resistance.

His voice, laden with unwavering resolve, sliced through the heavy tension. "I'll never bow to you, Zunga," he spat out, his gaze unflinching, a spark of rebellion burning fiercely in his eyes, unswayed and unbroken.

Scarlet, the embodiment of malevolence, took a menacing step closer, her eyes a fiery mix of anger and cruel satisfaction. The syringe became a weapon in her grip, and she wielded it with an air of malicious authority. In one swift motion, she drew the frog's DNA into the syringe, her fury and force merging into a vengeful act. The needle punctured the scientist's skin, injecting the mysterious substance.

A guttural howl of torment erupted from the scientist's lips as a profound transformation swept over him. His once-mighty form twisted and contorted, his body betraying him in a grotesque metamorphosis. No longer a panther, he was now a frog, an unthinkable change that left him as vulnerable as he was transformed.

The shocking revelation landed like a heavy blow. Lagartha's words hung in the air, leaving Hoppy with a mix of disbelief and realization. He turned to Greenie, his voice a mixture of astonishment and curiosity. "You used to be a panther?"

Greenie nodded, his voice carrying the weight of his transformation and the hidden layers of his past. "I was indeed a panther," he admitted, his words a bridge to the secrets he held. "The more I uncover, the more questions seem to surface," he confessed, his curiosity now a driving force pushing them forward.

"Is 'Greenie' your real name?" he ventured, the question holding layers of meaning that went beyond its simplicity.

With a knowing smile, Lagartha stepped in to answer. "Yes, it is," she confirmed, her voice tinged with the tenderness of someone who intimately knew the intricacies of Greenie's identity. "His fur was a deep, striking black, but when the light caught it just right, it gleamed with a stunning shade of green. His parents chose the name 'Greenie' to reflect both his unique appearance and his vibrant spirit."

"You too were a panther?" Hoppy's voice held a note of surprise.

Lagartha's reply was solemn, her gaze filled with a mixture of sorrow and empathy. "Yes," she answered, her voice carrying the weight of her own story.

Curiosity danced in Hoppy's eyes. "Then what happened?" he prodded, eager to hear more of the incredible tale.

Taking a deep breath, Greenie continued. "The pirates were just as baffled as you are now," he began. "When Zunga's gang saw me transform into a frog, their astonishment mirrored my own. It was a surreal moment, one that defied all reason and expectation."

"I was shocked myself," Greenie admitted, a wry smile playing on his lips. "My panther instincts were replaced with the unfamiliar sensations of being a frog."

He leaned in closer, his eyes locked with theirs, as he recounted the tumultuous events that unfolded. "As they lunged to catch me, my newfound frog agility became my greatest asset. I slipped through their grasps, zigzagging around them with quick hops that eluded their attempts to seize me."

Greenie's voice held the thrill of the chase. "I bounded and leaped with a swiftness and grace I had never known before. It was as though this transformed form had granted me an unexpected advantage."

A glint of determination flickered in his gaze as he relived his escape. "Amidst the mayhem, I caught sight of an open window. Without a second thought, I took a daring leap and found myself outside, beyond the pirates' reach."

"What about you, Lagartha?" Hoppy's voice held a hint of curiosity as he turned his attention to her. "Clearly, you're not dead."

Lagartha's eyes held a touch of nostalgia as she began to share her own remarkable transformation. "I transformed, much like Greenie," she began, her voice carrying a reminiscent undertone. "But my transformation was different, quieter, almost surreal."

Her words lingered in the air, pulling both Hoppy and Greenie into her narrative. "Shortly after they left in search of Greenie, something within me shifted. I woke up to a world that appeared different, felt different." Her gaze shifted, reliving the memory of that bewildering moment.

"I found myself transformed into a lizard," Lagartha continued, her voice resolute despite the oddity of her experience. "Confusion surrounded me as I struggled to make sense of my new form. I looked around, trying to comprehend what had just transpired."

A ghost of a smile graced her lips as she recollected the unexpected twist of fate. "And then, just as confusion settled in, Trigger entered the room. He and I share a history."

Hoppy's eyebrows arched in surprise. "Trigger? The massive tiger?"

Lagartha nodded, fondness shining in her eyes. "Yes, one and the same. He returned to check on my body, only to find it missing. Bewilderment shadowed his expression. I observed as he brought his paws to his face, his voice a mix of disbelief and frustration, muttering, 'What have you done?'"

A glint of determination sparkled in Lagartha's eyes. "In that moment, I knew I could trust him. I called out his name, and the shock in his eyes was unmistakable."

"Reem, is that really you?" Trigger's astonishment was palpable.

Lagartha's smile carried both nostalgia and fondness. "I asked him to look down, and there I stood—a lizard, a far cry from my original self."

The young kangaroo's expression held a mix of emotions. "So what did Trigger do then?"

Lagartha's voice held a note of warmth, carrying the weight of shared trust. "He was startled, but he quickly regained his composure. His eyes flickered with a mix of surprise and recognition. I told Trigger everything," Lagartha's tone held a blend of determination and emotion. "He explained that he had been stationed as a guard at the entrance, working alongside Zunga and the rest of the pirates."

Hoppy's expression was a tapestry of curiosity and comprehension. "Trigger sounds like he has a good heart."

Lagartha nodded, a touch of melancholy shading her eyes. "He truly does. But it's his brother, Stealheart, who chose the path of piracy. He was the one who led him astray."

"So, what did the two of you decide to do?"

Lagartha's gaze remained steady, unwavering. "We made the choice to keep my true identity hidden, revealing it only to our most trusted companions."

Hoppy's brows furrowed in thought, his curiosity piqued. "And what about Zunga and Stealheart?"

A bittersweet smile graced Lagartha's lips, a mix of emotions dancing in her eyes. "Trigger informed Stealheart that he had buried my body. It was a necessary falsehood to shield my true situation. And then, I embarked on a journey to locate Greenie."

"I found Greenie exactly where we had our first encounter," Lagartha recounted to Hoppy, her voice a blend of nostalgic reflection and unwavering purpose. "I had a strong intuition that he would seek refuge there. That place held special significance to him during his days as a panther."

Lagartha's gaze was adorned with the shimmer of memories. "Approaching him cautiously, I carried a whirlwind of emotions. I sensed that he had experienced something extraordinary, something beyond comprehension. And I had, too."

She paused, her eyes holding a sense of connection with Greenie. "Standing in front of him, I opened up about my own transformation. I revealed that I, too, had undergone a profound change shortly after he had left the lab, when he had turned into a frog."

The weight of their shared experiences hung in the air as Lagartha continued. "We exchanged our bewildered thoughts, trying to unravel the mysteries that had altered our very beings."

Hoppy leaned in, his curiosity piqued. "How did you feel, Greenie?"

A smile tugged at the corners of Greenie's lips. "I was stunned, as you can imagine. We were in this together. I held a mix of shock and relief, knowing that I wasn't alone in this strange transformation."

"We're here, Hoppy," Lagartha's voice came from under Hoppy's hat, bringing him back from the depths of her story. He looked up and saw the towering silhouette of the central bank building, bathed in the ethereal glow of the moonlight. Torches illuminated its façade, casting dancing shadows that seemed to whisper secrets of the night.

Caught between the enchanting scene and Lagartha's words, Hoppy's gaze lingered on the majestic structure. "It's something else," he murmured, a sense of awe in his voice.

Greenie, who shared in the admiration, chimed in with a nostalgic tone. "Indeed, it is. That building holds memories, stories of the past."

A wistful smile graced Greenie's lips as he gazed upon the grandeur before them. But reality quickly sobered their sentiments. "Now, though, it's fallen into the hands of pirates," he added, a note of concern in his voice.

Greenie's gaze shifted to the nearby garden, illuminated softly by the moonlight. "Hoppy, why don't you take a seat over there by the bench? We need to be cautious," he suggested, his eyes glancing towards the building's entrance. "Rocco might be inside," Hoppy said, his determination evident.

"Let's hope Trigger can provide us with the help we need to rescue Rocco," Greenie replied, his voice a mix of hope and uncertainty.

As they settled near the bench, Lagartha's eyes flickered towards the entrance. A figure caught their attention. "Look," she whispered, nodding toward the entrance. Trigger, with his powerful presence, was making his way towards the building, a determined stride in his gait.

Greenie's expression brightened. "It seems like Trigger is taking action," he said with a sense of relief, his confidence in their plan growing.

Together, they watched as Trigger's form disappeared into the building's entrance, their hearts filled with a mixture of anticipation and trepidation.

Deep within the heart of the central building, in Zunga's opulent office, a tense scene was unfolding. Rocco, his once vibrant feathers now dulled by captivity, was bound by a tight coil of rope, ensnared in Zunga's ruthless grip. The room was heavy with an air of intimidation, illuminated only by the soft glow of a flickering lamp.

Zunga's voice resonated with fury as he pressed his interrogation. "Where is that scientist frog, and what is his connection to the kangaroo?" His eyes bore into Rocco's, demanding answers.

Rocco, his heart racing, tried to muster his courage despite the dire circumstances. "I've only just met them," he managed to say, his voice wavering. "I don't know anything about where they might be."

A scowl twisted Zunga's features, his anger palpable. "You lie," he hissed, his patience wearing thin.

"We're friends now," Rocco protested, desperation edging into his voice. "Why would I lie to you?"

Zunga's fingers tightened around Rocco's feathers, a silent threat that hung heavily in the air. "Give me one good reason why I shouldn't squeeze the life out of you," he sneered, his gaze unrelenting.

Just then, a knock interrupted the tension in the room. "Come in," Zunga's voice snapped, his attention shifting to the door.

Trigger's massive form filled the doorway, his presence both commanding and unyielding. His fur carried an aura of quiet power, and his eyes held a steely determination. "Zunga," he said in his deep, resonant voice, "we need to talk."

Zunga's expression shifted from anger to surprise, a hint of wariness flickering in his eyes. "Trigger," he acknowledged, his tone guarded. "What do you want?"

"I am sailing in two days and need some entertainment," Trigger's unexpected request hung in the air, momentarily disarming the situation. "I was going to ask if I can borrow your canary."

Rocco, still ensnared by Zunga's grasp, saw an opportunity in Trigger's words. "That's a great idea," he chimed in, a glimmer of hope edging into his voice.

Zunga's gaze bore into Rocco, his reply measured and calculated. "This bird knows the scientist, Greenie," he emphasized, his grip on Rocco a chilling reminder of his control. Rocco swallowed hard, his throat working audibly in the charged atmosphere.

"Now talk, Bird," Zunga's demand cut through the tension, his eyes narrowing as he fixated on Rocco. "What's the relation Greenie has with the Kangaroo?" The question caught Trigger off-guard, a flicker of surprise betraying his thoughts. What did Zunga know? He exchanged a swift, uneasy glance with Rocco. How much had Zunga pieced together?

"Zunga, buddy, I've already told you," Rocco's voice held a note of exasperation, mixed with a touch of nervousness. "I only just met them."

Zunga's frustration was palpable. He walked over to an open window, his gaze sweeping the outside world as if contemplating the distance to the ground. The silence in the room was heavy, laden with the unspoken threat that lingered. "I am losing my patience, Bird," he warned, his tone chillingly matter-of-fact. "Either you talk, or I will drop you off."

With a calculated move, Zunga extended his arm out the window, taking Rocco with him. The bird's heart raced as he looked down, the ground seeming impossibly far away. His wings were bound, rendering him powerless against the fall. "For the last time, how do you know Greenie?" Zunga's voice held a mixture of anger and determination.

Trigger's mind raced. He couldn't afford to blow his cover, not now. He needed to protect Rocco. "Zunga," Trigger interjected, his tone measured, "this bird might have value alive. Information could be extracted—" Trigger's words were cut short by Zunga's dismissive wave. The pirate leader's eyes bore into Rocco, a chilling resolve emanating from him.

"Help, Help!" Rocco's urgent cry sliced through the stillness of the night, his voice ringing out into the darkness. The desperate plea reverberated, carrying his distress far and wide.

In an instant, Hoppy, Greenie, and Lagartha snapped their attention towards the source of the cry. Their eyes locked on the heart-pounding scene unfolding before them. High up in a window of the central building, Zunga stood with a twisted smile, a rope coiled menacingly around Rocco. The bird dangled in the air, his legs flailing helplessly as he fought to maintain his grip.

Hoppy's heart raced as he pointed toward the alarming sight. "Look! Zunga's got Rocco!"

Frustration burned in Zunga's eyes as he tightened his grip on the rope coiled around Rocco. His patience worn thin, he growled, "Enough of this!" With a sudden, callous move, he released his hold on Rocco. The bird's squawks of terror pierced the air as he plummeted toward the ground below.

Reacting swiftly, Hoppy's instincts kicked into overdrive. His muscles bunched as he sprang into action, his powerful legs propelling him forward. Underneath Hoppy's hat, Greenie and Lagartha clung on, their fingers digging into the fabric to ensure they stayed concealed and out of the wind.

The ground rushed beneath Hoppy's feet, and the world blurred into streaks of color as he built up an incredible speed. With a sudden shift, he veered towards the central building's garden, then defying gravity itself, he angled himself upwards. The wall of the towering structure became his path, a vertical trajectory that seemed impossible.

With each tap of his kangaroo tail against the building's surface, Hoppy managed to change his direction. His heart pounded as he zeroed in on Rocco, who was flailing through the air. The bird's cries for help turned into gasps of shock as Hoppy's arms closed around him. The momentum carried them upwards, defying Zunga's cruel intentions.

Zunga, his eyes wide with disbelief, watched the unexpected rescue unfold before him. He had expected Rocco to meet the ground, not be swept away by a determined kangaroo.

Rocco, his feathers ruffled and his heart racing, found himself safely cradled in Hoppy's grip. He managed a gasping chuckle as he peered up at his savior. "You really know how to make an entrance," he quipped, his relief palpable.

However, the speed had led them straight into an unforeseen challenge. Just as they approached the rooftop, an unexpected obstacle presented itself—a flagpole jutting from the building's side. With an inadvertent collision, Hoppy's forehead hit the pole, jarring him to an abrupt halt. His free hand shot out and grasped the edge of the roof, his fingers clinging to the precipice.

As Hoppy struggled to secure his grip, Rocco, still slightly dazed, gaped at the sudden turn of events. He managed a shaky laugh. "You've got to be kidding me," he muttered, a mix of awe and amusement in his voice. A brief kiss landed on Hoppy's cheek, a mixture of gratitude and sheer astonishment.

Summoning every ounce of strength, Hoppy hauled himself up to the rooftop, panting slightly from the exertion. Zunga's eyes bore into the scene, his surprise now replaced by a calculating glint. "Well, well," he murmured to himself. "This kangaroo might just be more trouble than I thought. Trigger, quick!" he barked, his voice laced with surprise and urgency. "The kangaroo is on the roof!"

Chapter Twelve

The Call

Perched atop the rooftop of the Central Building, Hoppy let out a relieved sigh. The adrenaline that had fueled his incredible feat was starting to ebb away, leaving behind a throbbing bump on his head. Beside him, Greenie emerged from under Hoppy's hat, his concerned gaze sweeping over Hoppy's form. Lagartha joined them, her eyes filled with both relief and urgency.

Greenie reached out to check on Hoppy, his fingers gently probing the bump. "You're alright?" he asked, his voice tinged with worry. Hoppy nodded, a slight grimace crossing his features. "Just a bit sore," he admitted.

Lagartha wasted no time, moving to untie the knots that had bound Rocco. The bird stretched his wings, offering a thankful chirp to Lagartha. "Thank you," Rocco said, his voice filled with genuine gratitude.

"We need to leave," Lagartha urged, her eyes scanning the rooftop for any signs of danger. But before they could make their move, the rooftop door swung open with a heavy creak, and Zunga strode out, flanked by Trigger. The air grew tense as their gazes locked onto the trio.

As if sensing the imminent threat, Zunga wasted no time. With a swift motion, he secured the door, sealing their fate on the rooftop. Without hesitation, Hoppy took action. He scooped up both Greenie and Lagartha and carefully placed them into the safety of his coat pocket. Meanwhile, Rocco launched himself into the sky, his wings carrying him to freedom.

Zunga barked orders at Trigger, his voice carrying the weight of his fury. "Get that kangaroo!" he commanded. Trigger nodded, his muscles tense with determination. Together, they advanced towards Hoppy, who knew he needed to act fast.

As they closed in, Hoppy sprang to his feet, his heart pounding in his chest. He had no clear plan, no destination in mind. He darted left and then right across the rooftop, his nimble movements causing Zunga and Trigger to adjust their trajectory. Hoppy's sprint became a dance, a desperate attempt to outmaneuver his pursuers.

But then, in a stroke of luck or perhaps fate's intervention, Hoppy spotted a flag fluttering from the back of the building. Another garden lay below, and at its center, an idea formed in Hoppy's mind. He dashed towards the edge, his speed reaching its peak. In a daring leap, he launched himself into the air.

For a moment, time seemed to slow. Hoppy's coat billowed behind him, creating the illusion of a makeshift cape. Zunga and Trigger stared in astonishment as Hoppy soared, his figure etched against the night sky. He stretched out his arms, aiming for a flagpole jutting from the garden.

With a heart-stopping grab, Hoppy snatched the pole, wrapping his legs around it to anchor himself. He descended with controlled grace, his descent slowed by the pole's firm hold. The impact with the ground was still jarring, and Hoppy winced as he hit the pavement.

Bruised and battered, Hoppy struggled to his feet, his breath coming in ragged gasps. But there was no time to rest. Rocco touched down nearby, his wings fluttering in worry.

"We need help," Greenie stated urgently. "Hoppy's hurt." Lagartha's eyes met Rocco's. "Go with him," Greenie instructed. "Find Dr. Silvershade. I'll stay with Hoppy," and without another word, the bird took off once more alongside Lagartha.

"Hoppy, can you walk?" Greenie's voice carried a sense of urgency, his eyes scanning Hoppy's condition. "We need to go. Zunga's not far behind, and he's likely bringing reinforcements this time."

Wincing, Hoppy managed to rise to his feet, though his movements were hindered by the pain in his side. He held his ribs tenderly, his face contorted in discomfort. "I'll try," he said through gritted teeth.

Greenie's concern was palpable as he cast a worried glance at Hoppy. "We can't stay here," he insisted, his voice edged with urgency. "Zunga's determined, and he won't give up until he's got us."

"I know," Hoppy replied, his breath uneven as he struggled to keep up with the others.

As they moved, the distant sounds of approaching pirates grew louder, a reminder of the danger that was closing in. "They're coming," Greenie warned, her gaze flicking towards the source of the noise.

Desperation took hold of Hoppy. "Greenie, you need to go," he panted, his words hurried. "Don't let them catch you."

Greenie hesitated, torn between staying with his friend and heeding the urgency of the situation. "I can't leave you," he protested, his eyes reflecting his inner turmoil.

"You have to," Hoppy insisted. "I'll slow them down. Just go, before it's too late."

With a heavy heart, Greenie nodded, his eyes locked onto Hoppy's. "Stay safe," he murmured before reluctantly slipping away, his form disappearing into the shadows.

The seconds ticked by like an eternity as the pirates drew closer. Zunga's figure emerged, accompanied by his entourage of raccoon servants, Trigger and Scarlet.

Zunga's gaze fixed on Hoppy, his eyes narrowing with a sinister gleam. Without warning, Zunga lunged forward, grabbing Hoppy by the arm and hurling him to the ground. The impact knocked the wind out of Hoppy, and he found himself pinned beneath Zunga's foot, struggling to breathe.

Zunga's voice dripped with malice as he leaned in, his face inches from Hoppy's. "What are you?" he hissed, the curiosity tinged with cruelty.

Hoppy's chest rose and fell as he gasped for air, his gaze unwavering. "I'm a walking kangaroo," he replied defiantly.

Zunga's lips curled into a cold smile. "And where's your friend Greenie?"

Hoppy's brow furrowed, his breaths coming in ragged gasps. "I don't know," he managed to utter, though his discomfort was evident.

Zunga's foot pressed down harder on Hoppy's chest, a mixture of anger and frustration crossing his features. "You're protecting him," he accused, the pressure intensifying.

Hoppy's muscles strained as he fought against Zunga's weight, his pain magnified by the mounting pressure. He clenched his teeth, determination fueling his efforts to push Zunga away.

Just as the situation seemed dire, a familiar voice rang out through the tension-filled air. "Leave him alone, Zunga. I'm here."

Greenie's defiant figure materialized from the shadows, his presence unwavering as he stepped forward, his eyes locked onto Zunga's. The air crackled with tension as the two adversaries faced off, their determination mirrored in their stances.

Zunga's lips curled into a sinister smile, his gaze shifting between Greenie and Hoppy. "Well, well, if it isn't the elusive panther," he purred, his tone laced with a mixture of amusement and intrigue.

Greenie's stance remained resolute, his eyes narrowed with unwavering resolve. "I won't let you hurt him," he declared, his voice steady and unyielding.

Zunga's voice cut through the tension like a blade. "Look at that, the frog still thinks he's a panther," he taunted, his leg pressing down on Hoppy's chest. The pressure was unrelenting, making each breath a struggle for Hoppy. Sweat glistened on his brow as he fought to endure the pain.

Greenie's heart raced as he watched the scene unfold before him. He knew that in his current form as a frog, he stood little chance against Zunga's overwhelming strength. But his determination burned bright in his eyes, a silent promise to protect his friend at any cost.

"What do you want, Zunga?" Greenie's voice held a mix of defiance and uncertainty. His hands clenched into fists, his body tense and ready for whatever might come next.

Zunga's grin widened, revealing a flash of sharp teeth. "Oh, don't play innocent, Greenie," he taunted. "Where did you hide the formula?" His gaze bore into Greenie, a dangerous glint in his eyes that sent a shiver down Greenie's spine.

Greenie's eyes narrowed, his mind racing. The formula was a double-edged sword, a power that could bring devastation as easily as salvation. He met Zunga's gaze with unwavering resolve. "Why are you doing this, Zunga?" he demanded, his voice laced with a mix of frustration and disbelief. "That formula is a threat. It has the potential to wipe out an entire country's crops and soil in mere minutes. Have you no concern for the lives you're endangering?"

Zunga's laughter echoed in response, devoid of remorse. "Lives? They're pawns in the grand game, Greenie," he sneered. "Power is what matters, and that formula is power."

Greenie's fists clenched at his sides, his frustration building. He couldn't let Zunga's ruthless pursuit of power go unchecked. "You're leading our island down a dangerous path," he argued, his voice heavy with a mix of anger and sorrow. "Is this really the legacy you want to leave behind?"

Zunga's expression remained unyielding, his gaze unwavering. "My legacy will be one of control and dominance," he declared coldly. "And you, Greenie, can either be a part of it or suffer the consequences."

Tension crackled in the air as the two locked in their verbal battle, their conflicting ideals and motives clashing against the backdrop of the moonlit garden. Meanwhile, Hoppy's struggle beneath Zunga's foot continued, a reminder of the immediate danger they all faced.

In the blink of an eye, a massive wolf leaped out from behind the trees, a powerful force that shattered the tense atmosphere. With a growl, the wolf lunged towards Zunga, pushing him away from Hoppy. The impact sent both of them tumbling across the ground, a swirl of dust and motion.

It was Dr. Silvershade, flanked by three other wolves, who had come to the rescue. The wolves moved with a coordinated precision, asserting their dominance over the situation. One swift female wolf managed to pin down the raccoon duo, Looney and Maroony, immobilizing them effectively.

In a blur of motion, another wolf closed in on Scarlet, the pirate fox, her dagger pressed against Scarlet's throat with a controlled intensity. Simultaneously, a male wolf moved like a shadow, deftly using a whip to ensnare Trigger, restricting his movements with practiced ease.

The area became an arena of fierce action, each movement calculated and executed with precision. Zunga and Dr. Silvershade locked in a battle of strength and will, grappling with each other as they fought for control. The clash of their power echoed in the night air, the ferocity of their struggle drawing the attention of everyone present.

But the fight took a turn as Zunga's raw strength began to overpower Dr. Silvershade. Their struggle intensified until it reached a climax, with Zunga's arm closing in around Dr. Silvershade's throat, choking the life out of him. The two adversaries wrestled on the ground, the tension between them reaching its peak.

Amidst the turmoil, a wolf's voice sliced through the chaos. "Let him go or I will end Scarlet's life," came the stern warning from the wolf who held the dagger to Scarlet's throat. Zunga's expression shifted, a flicker of uncertainty crossing his face. He understood the gravity of the situation – Scarlet was an integral part of his mission, and her life hung in the balance.

Reluctantly, Zunga released his grip on Dr. Silvershade, freeing him from his choking hold. The garden fell into a tense silence, the wolves maintaining their positions, ready to act at a moment's notice.

Dr. Silvershade's breaths came in heavy pants as he hoisted himself up off the ground, his eyes never leaving Hoppy who was struggling to his feet. "Hang in there, Hoppy," he urged, extending a steadying paw to the kangaroo. "We need to move."

Hoppy's determination was evident in the tight set of his jaw and the fire in his eyes. "Right, let's go," he responded with a mixture of resolve and urgency. With a swift motion, Greenie leaped onto Hoppy's tail, using it as a springboard to settle comfortably onto his shoulder, his focus keenly fixed on Zunga and the impending danger.

Zunga's venomous voice cut through the night air, his threats weaving a chilling promise of vengeance. "Remember this, the next time our paths cross, there won't be an ounce of mercy left," his tone dripped with malice. "I'll hunt each one of you down, relentlessly. And that formula, I'm going to seize it. Mark my words." Zunga's eyes locked onto their retreating figures, a sinister glint dancing in the moonlight.

The moon hung low in the sky as the group of wolves, Hoppy, and Greenie traversed through the dense forest, their steps guided by a mix of determination and a hint of weariness. The ancient trees seemed to whisper secrets as the wind rustled their leaves, creating a soft symphony of nature's voice.

After a while, the path led them to the mouth of a cavern nestled within the heart of a rocky outcrop. The entrance was shrouded in vines and moss, giving the impression of a hidden sanctuary. As the wolves and their companions entered, the interior of the cave revealed itself to be far from ordinary. Soft, glowing crystals adorned the walls, casting a gentle azure light that illuminated the space. The cave had been transformed into a haven, each corner carefully designed to exude warmth and comfort.

At the heart of this magical refuge, a room had been carved out to serve as Dr. Silvershade's home and practice. Books lined shelves that stretched towards the ceiling, ancient tomes filled with knowledge that spanned generations. A cozy seating area was adorned with plush cushions, inviting both conversation and relaxation.

As they made their way further into the cave, Dr. Silvershade's office came into view. A large wooden desk stood proudly in the center, scattered with papers, vials, and delicate instruments. Overhead, a collection of herbs and plants hung from the ceiling, their fragrance filling the air.

Seated on a comfortable couch were Rocco and Lagartha, their eyes lighting up as the group entered. The sight of familiar faces brought forth a collective sigh of relief, and warm smiles were exchanged all around. Rocco, perched on a cushion, fluffed his feathers in greeting. Lagartha, her wise eyes filled with a mixture of concern and relief, nodded to them all.

"Thank goodness you're safe," Lagartha said, her voice carrying a soothing reassurance.

Hoppy let out a tired chuckle, his ribs still aching from the earlier encounter. "We made it, thanks to you and the wolves."

Dr. Silvershade, his demeanor a mix of wisdom and kindness, approached with a soothing potion. "Hoppy, let's tend to those bruises," he said, his eyes meeting Hoppy's with a comforting gaze.

Greenie perched on a nearby ledge, his emerald eyes reflecting gratitude. "We owe you and your pack a great deal," he said, his words carrying sincerity.

One of the wolves, a gentle yet imposing figure, stepped forward. "We couldn't stand by while you faced danger," the wolf spoke, her voice laced with a quiet strength. "We are united against the threat Zunga poses."

Greenie's words of gratitude to Kowkab, the female wolf, resonated in the cavernous space. "Thank you, Kowkab," he said with a genuine smile, his eyes reflecting the appreciation he felt.

As the group settled into the cave, Hoppy found himself sinking into a cushioned mossy nook, a makeshift bed that felt surprisingly comfortable. The events of the night had left him physically drained, and the coolness of the cave provided a welcome relief from the tension outside. The wolves moved with a quiet grace, finding their own spots to rest, their presence a comforting reminder of their protection.

Kowkab, her silver fur glinting in the soft light, turned to Dr. Stealheart, her mate. Her eyes held a mixture of concern and anticipation. "What do we do now?" she asked him, a subtle edge of worry in her voice.

Dr. Silvershade, the steady force among them, spoke up. "Now, we rest," he said, his tone both reassuring and practical. "Hoppy's taken quite a beating, and we could all use some time to recuperate. Tomorrow will bring its own set of challenges."

Kowkab's gaze shifted toward Hoppy, her maternal instincts apparent. "I'll prepare a little something to snack on," she said. "You must be hungry after all that running and fighting."

Hoppy couldn't help but smile at the thought of food. "That sounds great," he said, his voice tinged with gratitude. "I think I could definitely use a snack right now."

Greenie's expression turned serious as he leaned in, his eyes flickering with a mixture of determination and concern. "Zunga won't give up easily," he said, his words a reminder of the looming

195

threat. "He's relentless, and he'll stop at nothing to get what he wants."

Dr. Silvershade nodded in agreement. "You're right, Greenie," he said. "But for now, let's put that aside and focus on recovering. We'll discuss our next steps in the morning."

A sense of calm settled over the cave as the group gathered together, the glow of the crystals casting intricate patterns on the walls. The tension of the night began to ease, replaced by a shared understanding that they were safe for the moment.

"I've already sent my son, Noawf, to let Philip know what happened tonight," Dr. Silvershade continued. "As of now, we're under the radar, and this cave offers us protection."

The conversations slowly tapered off as Kowkab returned with a simple spread of fruits, bread and nuts. The group ate in companionable silence, the flickering light from the crystals casting a warm glow over their faces. The world outside seemed distant, the concerns of the night momentarily set aside as the group found solace in each other's company.

A sense of tranquility prevailed as Dr. Silvershade meticulously prepared a soothing herbal paste for Hoppy's bruises. The gentle rustling of leaves and the distant sound of a bubbling brook outside added to the serene ambiance. "This should help ease the discomfort," Dr. Silvershade assured Hoppy, applying the paste with a gentle touch.

Hoppy offered a grateful smile, feeling the cooling effect of the herbs on his sore skin. "Thanks, Doc," he said, his voice carrying a mix of relief and appreciation.

Rocco, his fatigue finally catching up to him, had already succumbed to sleep. His rhythmic breathing served as a backdrop to the cave's calm.

Dr. Silvershade attended to Hoppy's minor wounds with meticulous care, his nimble hands working with a mix of expertise and compassion. Meanwhile, Kowkab, a vigilant wolf with a keen sense of duty, positioned herself near the cave's entrance. Her watchful eyes scanned the surrounding landscape, every rustle of leaves or distant sound met with her unwavering attention. At her side sat Dr. Stealheart, her loyal mate, their united presence emanating a silent aura of security for the group.

As the first tendrils of dawn stretched across the horizon, a soft radiance began to fill the cave. In this delicate light, Lagartha stirred from her slumber, her eyes adjusting to the gradually brightening surroundings. She rose gracefully, her movements purposeful and unhurried, and approached Kowkab.

"Morning," Lagartha greeted in a hushed tone, her urgency apparent. "I need to make my way to the bar. It won't be functioning properly without my guidance, and I have to disseminate information and alert the moles about the events of last night."

Kowkab nodded, her understanding mirrored in her gaze. "Take care, Lagartha," she cautioned, her words tinged with a motherly concern. "The world outside can be unpredictable."

Lagartha's smile held a mixture of determination and confidence. "No worries, blending in is something I've mastered," she replied with self-assuredness. "Last night, Zunga and his crew were none the wiser."

With that assurance, Kowkab turned her attention back to her sentinel duty, her watchful gaze resuming its steadfast vigil. Lagartha, resolute and focused, slipped out of the cave and embraced the embrace of the early morning light.

The day unfolded gradually, the sun's rays painting the landscape with shades of gold and green. Inside the cave, Hoppy's bruises began to feel better, and the sense of camaraderie among the group grew stronger.

As the morning sun painted the sky with warm hues, Nowaf made his way back to the cave, his steps light but purposeful. He had spent the previous night at Philip's, delivering the crucial information about the events that had unfolded. The island's fate rested heavily on their shoulders, and Nowaf's mind was abuzz with thoughts as he approached the cave.

Carrying a woven basket filled with a simple but hearty breakfast, Nowaf entered the cave to find the group gathered and ready to start the day. The scent of freshly baked bread and a hint of herbs filled the air, eliciting appreciative murmurs from his companions. He distributed the food, and they ate with a mixture of hunger and gratitude, knowing that their alliance was their greatest strength.

As the meal concluded, Dr. Silvershade cleared his throat. "Greenie," he said, gesturing toward his office area, "Come with me. I want to show you something."

Greenie followed the doctor into the cozy, well-organized section of the cave that served as both living space and workspace. On a sturdy wooden table, a collection of vials, papers, and tools were meticulously arranged. Dr. Silvershade had been tirelessly working on a formula to reverse the mutation that had turned Greenie into a frog.

Dr. Silvershade picked up a vial filled with a shimmering liquid. "I've made significant progress," he began, "but there's a missing piece. We need some kind of DNA from your panther form."

Greenie examined the vial, his brow furrowed in thought. "DNA from when I was a panther?" he echoed, considering the possibilities.

"Yes," Dr. Silvershade affirmed, "some trace of your panther self that can help us create a formula tailored to your specific transformation."

Greenie's mind raced, memories of his panther days flooding back. "I remember the lush forest, the scent of the leaves, the feel of the cool earth beneath my paws," he mused aloud. "But how do we find a suitable DNA sample?"

Dr. Silvershade nodded thoughtfully. "That's where you come in," he said, a hint of a smile tugging at his lips. "Your keen memory and understanding of your panther self can guide us. We need something that captures the essence of that time."

Their faces reflecting a mixture of curiosity and determination, Greenie's voice broke the silence, his eyes fixed on Dr. Silvershade. "and Lagartha's DNA... how can we even find it? Locating our DNA from eight years ago does not look promising."

Dr. Silvershade leaned forward, his eyes locking onto Greenie's. "That's where the magic comes in," he explained. "I managed to secure a copy of the ancient Magic Book, often referred to as The Opening Book among the rat community."

"The Opening Book?" Greenie's eyebrows shot up in surprise.

Dr. Silvershade nodded, his expression serious yet hopeful. "Indeed. This book is said to hold spells that only rats with innate magical abilities can access. With its power, we may be able to delve into your memories and retrieve your original forms temporarily. The book requires a specific spell, one that requires a powerful source of magic to enact."Zatarh has mastered the arts of magic. With her expertise, we might have a chance at casting the spell and obtaining the samples we need."

Greenie leaned forward, his eyes reflecting determination. "But rescuing Zatarh from Zunga, that's another challenge entirely."

Dr. Silvershade's gaze grew intense. "Indeed. Zunga will do whatever it takes to use her powers for his own gains."

Outside the cave, the morning sun painted the landscape with soft hues of gold and pink, and a gentle breeze rustled through the leaves. Hoppy, Rocco, and Kowkab sat on the grassy ledge, gazing out at the breathtaking view before them. The distant sound of waves crashing against the shore provided a soothing backdrop to their conversation.

Rocco's eyes scanned the horizon as he pondered their next steps. "So, what's the plan now?"

Kowkab's eyes sparkled as she leaned back, taking in the scene. "We wait. Our friends will be here soon. We're not alone in this."

Curiosity got the better of Hoppy, and he turned to Kowkab with an inquisitive expression. "Kowkab, I've never known Greenie as a panther. What was he like back then?"

Kowkab's gaze softened as if reminiscing about a distant memory. "Greenie, or should I say, 'Panther Greenie,' was truly something. His presence commanded respect, and his fur would shimmer like emerald under the sunlight. Despite his brilliance, he remained humble, never one to boast about his achievements."

Hoppy's eyes widened in surprise. "Brilliant? In what way?"

Kowkab chuckled. "He was an aspiring scientist, even from a young age. I remember he built an intricate model ship as a teenager, a replica of what would become the legendary Red Carrack."

Recognition lit up Hoppy's eyes. "The Red Carrack? That's the ship that brought us here."

Kowkab nodded with a warm smile. "Indeed, and when Greenie reached adulthood, he turned his dream into reality. The Red Carrack became a vessel for exploring the unknown, uncovering history's secrets, and seeking hidden treasures." Kowkab's eyes sparkled as she recalled those times. "The camaraderie among the crew was unparalleled. We faced challenges, laughed, and bonded as a family. The Red Carrack symbolized adventure, knowledge, and unity."

The sun had climbed higher in the sky, casting a warm glow over the scene as they continued their conversation. Kowkab adjusted her position, settling in to share the story of Greenie's past.

Hoppy's curiosity got the better of him, and he turned to Kowkab with a thoughtful expression. "Kowkab, can I ask you something? Why did Greenie and Lagartha split?"

Rocco's eyebrows shot up in surprise. "Wait, they were married? I had no idea."

Kowkab offered a sympathetic smile. "Yes, they were. Their story is a complex one, but it's rooted in a love that transformed over time."

She leaned back, her gaze fixed on a distant memory. "Greenie and Lagartha were young and deeply in love when they first met. They both shared a passion for discovery and adventure, and their relationship blossomed as they explored the mysteries of the world together."

Rocco's eyes softened as he listened intently. "So, what happened?"

Kowkab's tone grew reflective. "As time went on, their paths began to diverge. Greenie became increasingly absorbed in his scientific pursuits, while Lagartha's heart yearned for exploration beyond the laboratory. Their differences led to growing tension, and they realized that their dreams were pulling them in different directions."

Hoppy's eyes held a mixture of understanding and curiosity. "Did their separation cause bad tension between them?"

Kowkab shook her head, her expression gentle. "Not at all. In fact, their bond remained unbreakable. They realized that while their romantic relationship had evolved, their deep friendship endured. They decided to part ways amicably, preserving the precious connection they shared."

Rocco's gaze drifted to the horizon, lost in thought. "That's quite a mature way to handle things."

Kowkab nodded, her eyes filled with a sense of admiration. "Indeed, it was a testament to their maturity and the deep respect they had for each other. While they pursued their individual paths, their friendship continued to thrive. They became each other's confidantes, offering unwavering support in the face of challenges."

The trio sat in contemplative silence for a moment, the weight of the past hanging in the air. The breeze whispered through the trees, carrying with it a sense of nostalgia and understanding.

"We've all grown and changed since then," Kowkab mused, breaking the silence. "But their story reminds us that love can transform into different shapes, yet remain a powerful force that binds us together."

Kowkab's curious gaze fixed on Hoppy, a genuine interest sparkling in her eyes.

"I heard you have a remarkable ability, Hoppy," Kowkab said, her tone laced with intrigue. "Not only are you a walking Kangaroo, but you have astonishing speed."

Rocco's eyes lit up, a mischievous grin playing on his lips. "Oh, you should've seen him last night! It was like watching a blur."

Hoppy chuckled, his cheeks slightly flushed from the attention. "Well, I did have a bit of practice."

Rocco leaned forward, eager to share his version of the story. "So, last night, Zunga had Hoppy cornered on the rooftop, right? And then, out of nowhere, Hoppy just zooms past him like lightning and glides down like some sort of superhero."

Kowkab's laughter chimed like a melodic bell, adding to the lighthearted atmosphere. "My, my, that must have been quite the sight."

Amid the laughter, Hoppy's expression turned more contemplative. "You know, it's funny how things turn out. I wasn't always so confident in my abilities."

Rocco raised an eyebrow, intrigued. "What do you mean?"

A wistful smile graced Hoppy's lips as he delved into his past. "When I was just a young kangaroo, my family treated me like I was... well, different. My mom worried that others would make fun of me. So, I was home-schooled, and I could only play in the front yard at night, never alone. As I grew older, the rules did not change."

Kowkab's expression softened, her empathy palpable. "That must've been really tough."

Hoppy nodded, his eyes reflecting a mix of emotions. "It was. I felt trapped and isolated, and there were times when I couldn't help but cry. But then, one day, I made the decision to leave all of that behind. I wanted to find my own path, to prove that I was more than just my differences."

Rocco leaned in closer, engrossed in Hoppy's story. "And that's when you met Greenie, right?"

Hoppy's eyes lit up with a mixture of gratitude and fondness. "Yes, that's when our paths crossed. Greenie saved my life when I was in a dangerous situation. He didn't see me as different or strange. He saw potential in me."

Kowkab's smile reflected the warmth of Hoppy's story. "It sounds like he saw the real you."

Hoppy nodded, his heart full. "Exactly. Greenie showed me that being unique isn't something to be ashamed of. It's something to embrace and use for good."

Kowkab's eyes were kind and understanding as she listened. She was also eager to know more about Rocco's past.

"So, Rocco, what's your story?" Kowkab inquired gently, her voice inviting Rocco to share his own journey.

Rocco leaned back, gathering his thoughts before he began to speak. "Well, it all started with my family back in Bermany. I had a wonderful mother and two older siblings, a brother and a sister. I was the youngest of the bunch."

He closed his eyes momentarily, lost in the memories of his childhood. "We lived in a stunning tree home, two stories tall. Each of us had our own room on the second floor, one in each corner. Our family was close-knit, and we would often embark on trips and camping adventures together."

Rocco's expression softened as he continued his tale. "But things took a turn when my father left us one day and never returned. Our lives changed after that. Then, one tragic day, a fire engulfed our tree home along with many others. It was devastating. We lost everything."

Kowkab's gaze reflected empathy as Rocco spoke of the challenges he faced. "I can't imagine what that must have been like."

Rocco's gaze shifted to the flickering shadows dancing the trees. "After the fire, my mother's spirit seemed to break. She grew weaker, and not long after, she passed away. It was just me and my siblings left."

He continued, his voice tinged with a mix of sorrow and resilience. "My sister found love with wealthy canary and left to start her own family. My brothers, they started a nut business together. They were always best of friends. As for me, well, I discovered that I had a knack for music."

A wistful smile crept onto Rocco's face as he recalled his musical pursuits. "I learned to hustle using my musical talents. Street performances, gigs at local cafes—I did whatever it took to make ends meet."

Kowkab's eyes held a mixture of admiration and sympathy. "You've been through a lot, Rocco."

Rocco nodded, his gaze thoughtful. "Yeah, life has thrown its challenges, but I've learned to adapt and find my way. And now, here I am, part of this eclectic group of friends."

Hoppy turned his attention to Kowkab, his eyes reflecting genuine interest. "Kowkab," he began, "what's the story behind Zatara?"

Rocco's eyes brightened with a flash of recognition, a flicker of memory igniting within him. Ah, yes, he recalled. Zatara – back when they were both ensnared in the dark clutches of that foreboding ship's dungeon – had entrusted him with a vital message. The weight of that responsibility settled firmly on his shoulders as he mused on her words.

Kowkab smiled warmly, her eyes reflecting a fond familiarity with the tale she was about to share. "Ah, Zatara," she began, her voice carrying a tone of respect. "She is indeed a remarkable figure in the world of magic."

The group gathered closer, anticipation palpable in the air. Kowkab continued, her words weaving a vivid tapestry of magic and mystery. "You see, all witches in our world are rats, but not all rats are witches. Zatara, along with her two sisters—Farara and Taoona—are masters of the magic arts. They come from a unique culture and a land of their own, a place where magic is woven into the very fabric of their lives."

As Kowkab spoke, the others could almost picture the enchanting world that Zatara and her sisters hailed from—a realm where spells danced on the air and secrets were whispered in ancient incantations. "Zatara was chosen to be their leader," Kowkab continued. "Her sisters joined her in this leadership, forming a powerful trio that held the keys to the magic world's secrets."

Her voice carried a blend of admiration and reverence as she delved into the past. "Many years ago, they worked tirelessly to be known beyond their own borders. Zatara and her sisters embarked on journeys to meet with leaders from different parts of our planet. They showcased their knowledge, their wisdom, and their remarkable leadership skills."

Kowkab's gaze seemed to travel to distant memories as she painted a picture of a world in transformation. "Leaders from various countries were astounded by Zatara's insights, her ability to unite different nations, and her commitment to fostering peace." Her words held a touch of wonder, as if the events she described still held a touch of magic.

"They managed to bring several countries together," Kowkab continued, her voice tinged with a sense of awe. "Under Zatara's guidance, they forged alliances, embraced diversity, and walked a path of understanding. It was a time when differences were set aside for the greater good."

The atmosphere was thick with anticipation as the group huddled closer, drawn by the intrigue of the tale she was about to unveil.

"Picture the rats sailing under the inky canvas of a moonlit night. The waves whispered their secrets, and the stars above held timeless tales."

Rocco's eyes were wide, his imagination painting vivid scenes of the rat sisters on their journey. "And then what happened?"

Kowkab's whiskers quivered, revealing her own excitement for the tale. "As night unfurled its veil, slumber settled upon Zatara, Farara, and Taoona. In that realm between reality and dreams, something extraordinary occurred."

Hoppy leaned forward, "Tell us!"

Kowkab's voice carried them into the heart of the dream. "They shared a dream, as if their minds intertwined through the threads of magic. In this dream, a figure emerged—a creature both strange and yet eerily familiar."

Hoppy's brows furrowed with intrigue. "A creature? What kind?"

Kowkab's gaze seemed to look beyond the hills, into the past where the story unfolded. "They described it as an ape-like being, possessing an air of wisdom and enigma that defied their understanding. Its presence exuded a mix of ancient knowledge and unfathomable secrets."

As Kowkab's words wove the dream into reality, the cave seemed to shiver with a different kind of energy. "So, what did this ape-like figure do in the dream?" Rocco asked, leaning forward.

Kowkab's eyes sparkled with the dream's mysteries. "It spoke to them—across the boundaries of dreams and reality. Its voice held echoes of distant realms and ages past. And, in each dream, it revealed the same thing."

The group leaned in, caught in the web of anticipation. "The same thing? What was it?" Hoppy's curiosity hung in the air like a question mark.

"In every dream," Kowkab said, her voice low and evocative, "the figure unveiled the location of a powerful yellow diamond."

Rocco's eyes widened in awe. "Yellow diamond?

Kowkab nodded. Indeed. And the dreams weren't a one-time occurrence. They came to Zatara, Farara, and Taoona five times, each time guiding them to the hidden places where these diamonds rested.

"They were being shown the locations of these precious gems?" Hoppy's voice was laced with curiosity, his mind working to grasp the depth of the story.

Kowkab's nod was like a nod from destiny itself. "Yes, each dream was like a chapter, revealing a map to these four diamonds of immeasurable power."

The sunlight danced on Kowkab's fur as she continued her mesmerizing tale, her words spinning a vivid tapestry of events that captured the imagination of her rapt audience.

"After receiving these dreams," Kowkab's voice held a tinge of gravity, "Zatara, Farara, and Taoona were compelled to embark on a quest—a daring expedition to confirm the reality behind their shared visions."

Hoppy leaned in, his eyes gleaming with intrigue. "And did they find the diamond?"

Kowkab's whiskers twitched with a hint of a smile. "Indeed, they did. Guided by the clues woven within their dreams, the sisters and their chosen team of intrepid rats set out to the location they had seen in their slumber. With determination and curiosity as their guides, they unearthed the radiant treasure—the first of the four powerful yellow diamonds."

The group's eyes shone with wonder, a collective breath held in anticipation of the story's twists and turns. "So, they brought the diamond back to their home?" Rocco's voice was eager, his mind weaving a picture of the daring adventure.

Kowkab's gaze held a mixture of pride and somberness. "Yes, the diamond was returned to their haven—a place where magic and wisdom flowed freely. They believed the diamond held secrets and potential beyond measure, and so they studied it, unlocking some of its enchantments. But they were betrayed."

"But then," Hoppy's voice held a note of concern, "betrayal?"

Kowkab's expression darkened, her voice weaving a somber thread through the intimate ambiance of the cave. "Indeed, it's a tale woven with threads of light and shadow, hope intertwined with betrayal. Among the rats, a figure named Eldrak held the sisters' trust—a rat of ancient wisdom, a master of elusive magic."

Rocco's brows knitted together, a blend of curiosity and concern furrowing his features. "And did this Eldrak, the trusted one, turn against them?"

Kowkab's gaze held a weighty mixture of sadness and determination. "Yes, he did. Eldrak, lured by the seductive promise of power and dominion, forged an unholy alliance with the pirates who plagued our island."

A sense of disbelief tinged Hoppy's voice. "But how could he betray his own kind?"

Kowkab's eyes reflected a complex tapestry of emotions. "Ambition, greed, the allure of forbidden knowledge—these are the snares that ensnare even the noblest of hearts. Eldrak's fall into darkness serves as a stark reminder that the most brilliant lights can cast the deepest shadows."

"So," Hoppy's voice held thoughtful ponderance, "the one they held in highest regard became their ultimate adversary?"

Kowkab's nod was filled with a collective understanding shared among the group. "Indeed, the betrayal of Eldrak shattered their trust, casting a long shadow over their journey—a journey fraught with challenges beyond the mere pursuit of diamonds."

"Is Eldrak the reason why Zunga possesses one of the diamonds?" Hoppy's gaze fixed on Kowkab, his curiosity ablaze.

Kowkab's response was laden with the weight of truth. "Yes," she confirmed, her voice steady with revelation. "Eldrak's treachery, a mastery of deception and betrayal, paved the way for Zunga's possession of one of the diamonds."

Rocco's eyes widened as he grappled with the implications of this connection. "So, that traitorous rat played a pivotal role in all of this?" he interjected, a mixture of incredulity and indignation coloring his words.

Kowkab's gaze wove together threads of sorrow and understanding, her words carrying the weight of a tale intricately spun. "Indeed, Rocco," she affirmed, her voice a steady guide through the labyrinth of history. "Eldrak's insatiable thirst for power and his willingness to dance with darkness led him down a treacherous path—one that converged with Zunga's ambitious designs."

A contemplative hush draped over the cave, the narrative's gravity settling upon the listeners like a cloak of uncertainty. Amidst this atmospheric stillness, Hoppy's voice arose like a beacon, seeking further illumination. "But you mentioned five dreams, and yet there are only four diamonds?" His words sliced through the quiet, drawing the group deeper into the story's embrace.

Kowkab's countenance turned introspective, as if she herself journeyed back in time. "Yes, five dreams," her tone held a thoughtful cadence, the melody of her voice resonating with the intrigue of untold secrets. "The sisters, driven by an unquenchable thirst for uncovering the diamonds' mysteries, chose to channel their unique gifts."

With rapt attention, the group leaned in, drawn by the enigmatic revelations unfurling before them. "In the fifth and final dream," Kowkab's words carried a rhythmic current, weaving through the very fabric of the story, "the sisters embraced audacity. They granted Eldrak access to their dreamscape, allowing him to peer through their eyes."

A collective breath, as if suspended in time, hung in the air—a pause laden with the tale's weight. "And what did Eldrak witness?" Hoppy's question lingered like a chord waiting to resolve, an echo that demanded to be heard.

Kowkab's gaze met each pair of eyes, her voice a beacon guiding them further into the story's heart. "Through their shared dream, Eldrak did not witnessed the locations of the diamonds but only the incredible potential they held—how they could access the elusive black gold, a substance of immense power and danger."

Kowkab's gaze remained steady, her voice resonating with the echoes of the past. "He reported the vision the sisters had to the pirates—Zunga and his crew. The vision depicted an advanced civilization on a planet similar to our own, a civilization capable of extracting the enigmatic black gold from deep within their world."

Hoppy's eyes widened in realization. "They saw how to harness the power of the black gold."

Kowkab nodded solemnly. "Exactly. Eldrak shared details of a planet that held vast reservoirs of this black gold, hidden within its very core. It was said to possess the power to manipulate energies and reshape the very fabric of reality. But with great power comes great risk, and Eldrak warned the pirates that tapping into this black gold could also bring harm to the planet itself."

Hoppy's brows furrowed, his mind connecting the dots. "The yellow diamonds are the key."

Kowkab's gaze met his, a mixture of somber wisdom in her eyes. "Indeed. Eldrak unveiled the pivotal role of the yellow diamonds—they held the ability to drill to the core of our planet, a feat no other substance could achieve. To harness the black gold's potential, they needed the power of three yellow diamonds."

A hush fell over the group, the implications of this revelation sinking in. "So, Eldrak told the pirates the sisters knew where the diamonds were?" Rocco's question hung in the air.

Kowkab's expression darkened, her voice tinged with a sense of bitterness. "Yes. Eldrak revealed the location of the yellow diamond the sisters had discovered. He also made known that Zatara and her sisters held the knowledge of the other diamonds' whereabouts."

Hoppy's fists clenched, a mixture of anger and frustration welling up within him. "And then they stole the diamond and captured Zatara."

Kowkab's eyes reflected the pain of the past, "Indeed. The pirates seized the diamond and captured Zatara, holding her hostage to force her sisters into submission. But the sisters were not defenseless—they vanished into hiding, protected by their peers, seeking refuge from the impending storm."

"Does anyone know where Zatara's sisters are?" Hoppy's voice broke the silence, his eyes searching Kowkab's for any hint of an answer.

Kowkab's expression bore a blend of worry and determination as she replied, "We don't know their exact location. But finding them before the pirates do is crucial."

A moment of contemplative silence hung over them until Rocco's voice, strong and resolute said, "Actually, I know where they are."

The statement caused a ripple of astonishment, and Hoppy leaned in, his curiosity piqued. "How do you know, Rocco?"

Rocco met their gazes, his eyes holding a mix of memories. "Zatara told me. Back when we were both locked up in that wretched ship's dungeon. It kind of slipped my mind in all the chaos, but she wanted me to pass on a message to Lagartha. She wanted her to know that her sisters are safe and their whereabouts are known."

A mix of relief and confusion swept across their faces, and Hoppy's question was laced with a touch of reproach. "Why didn't you tell us this earlier?"

Rocco sighed, a hint of weariness in his voice. "Haven't you seen what I've been through? My mind was a jumble of thoughts, and this piece of information got pushed to the back. I'm just glad I remembered now."

Kowkab's eyes gleamed with a glimmer of hope. "This is good news indeed. We can finally work towards reuniting Zatara with her sisters and gather their strength against Zunga."

A gentle breeze rustled the leaves overhead, filling the air with a symphony of whispers from the trees. The companions, now seated in a loose circle on the soft grass, felt the anticipation humming in the air.

Kowkab's ears perked up, her keen wolf senses attuned to a subtle shift in the environment. Her gaze sharpened as she turned her attention towards the mouth of the cave, where the dense undergrowth gave way to a path leading into the forest. Rocco's brow furrowed, his curiosity piqued. "What is it, Kowkab?"

With a mix of excitement and certainty, Kowkab replied, "They've arrived."

The words hung in the air like a promise, and the clearing seemed to come alive with a renewed energy. Just then, emerging from the shadows of the forest, Philip the wise owl swooped gracefully into view. His wings beat with a rhythmic grace as he settled on a nearby branch, his wise eyes glistening in the light.

Following Philip's lead, the forest seemed to come alive with movement. Monkeys swung through the trees, their agile forms leaping from branch to branch with joyful abandon. A pair of leopards padded into the clearing, their sleek muscles rippling beneath their spotted coats. Nearby, apes gathered, their intelligent eyes taking in the scene before them.

A majestic bear lumbered forward, its massive form a testament to the raw power of nature. A group of squirrels scampered in, their tiny paws carrying them with a flurry of energy. And finally, with a deliberate and unhurried pace, Lamar the wise koala made his appearance, his calm demeanor radiating a sense of serenity.

Kowkab's tail wagged in excitement, her wolf instincts telling her that this gathering was a significant moment; a sense of unity threading through the air.

As the diverse group of allies settled into the clearing, Hoppy and Rocco exchanged delighted glances. The companions could hardly contain their joy at the sight of this unexpected support arriving in swift response to their call. The forest seemed to echo with the soft rustling of leaves and the soothing melodies of birdsong, bearing witness to the beginning of a new chapter in their journey.

With the golden hues upon the horizon, the echoes of the past still reverberated through the minds of our heroes. As they stood together, united by a shared purpose, a new chapter of their journey awaited. The mysteries of the diamonds, the secrets of the black gold, and the battles yet to be fought were etched in their determined gazes.

But as the final pages of this tale came to a close, a tantalizing promise lingered in the air—a promise of further revelations, daring exploits, and unforeseen twists. The story of Hoppy and his companions was far from over, and the adventures that lay ahead would test their mettle, forge unbreakable bonds, and unveil truths that could reshape their world.

As the last words were read, a simple yet powerful phrase emerged, a promise to readers young and old, igniting their anticipation and leaving them hungry for what comes next:

"To Be Continued..."

About the Author

Ahmed Andridge is a unique individual, whose life journey spans across continents, cultures, and experiences, shaping him into the multifaceted person he is today. Born on January the 5th in Alexandria, Virginia, Ahmed's early life was one of international diplomacy and exposure. His father's career as a diplomat led Ahmed to experience diverse environments, from the USA to the USSR and eventually back to his ancestral homeland in Ras al-Khaimah, United Arab Emirates. With an Emirati father and a Syrian mother, he navigated a unique blend of influences that shaped his outlook on life.

Having spent his formative years in Ras al-Khaimah, UAE, Ahmed's childhood was marked by the rich Emirati heritage and the rapidly changing landscape of a developing nation. As the UAE transitioned from independent Emirates to a modern state, Ahmed's father, a witness to this transformation, instilled in him a deep sense of pride in his Emirati heritage. This sense of heritage, coupled with his upbringing in both the UAE and the United States, fostered Ahmed's appreciation for diversity, community, and the importance of education.

Ahmed's upbringing, marked by cultural shifts and adaptability, fostered a unique perspective that bridged his Emirati heritage with the American upbringing he received. His educational journey was rich and diverse, with stints in American and international schools, where he developed his linguistic and cognitive skills.

His professional journey unfolded with success in the automotive industry, where he started as a technician and ascended to become a master technician at BMW. His entrepreneurial spirit led him to establish his own independent BMW repair shop, which flourished into a successful venture. Despite personal setbacks, such as the loss of his spouse, Ahmed displayed a remarkable capacity for adaptation and reinvention. He expanded his endeavors into various businesses, ranging from antiques to classic car restoration.

But Ahmed's story is not just about personal achievements; it's also about community and giving back. His commitment to fostering connections, sharing knowledge, and supporting others is evident in his establishment of the Atlanta City Soccer Club. As a coach and administrator for young athletes, he imparts not only the skills of the game but also valuable life lessons.

Ahmed's life story embodies the convergence of diverse cultures, unwavering determination, resilience, and an unyielding commitment to both personal growth and community betterment. His journey serves as an inspiration, reflecting the power of human adaptability and the profound impact that one individual can have on the lives of many. Through his experiences, Ahmed Andridge has become a living testament to the importance of embracing change, learning from adversity, and living a life deeply intertwined with the values of community, education, and empathy.